POKER
SOULLESS KINGS MC: MARBLE FALLS, TX

ANDI RHODES

BLUE JOURNEY PUBLISHING

Copyright © 2025 by Andi Rhodes

All rights reserved.

No part of this book may be reproduced in any form or by any electronic or mechanical means, including information storage and retrieval systems, without written permission from the author, except for the use of brief quotations in a book review.

This is a work of fiction and the product of the author's imagination. All names, characters, businesses, places, events and incidents are used in a fictitious manner, unless otherwise noted. Any resemblance to actual persons, living or deceased, or actual events is purely coincidental.

Cover Artwork - © Dez Purington at Pretty in Ink Creations

Editing - Darcie Fisher at Into the Gray Author Services

A NOTE FROM THE AUTHOR:

Welcome back to the world of the Soulless Kings MC: Marble Falls, TX chapter! This is Poker and Meri's story. I must confess, I had an entirely different plan and woman for Poker, and then Meri came along in Ghost (you don't have to have read Ghost to enjoy this story, but really, you know you want to 😉), and I knew she was Poker's 'one'.

Surprisingly, there aren't really any triggering topics in this book, unless you count the actions of one-percenters triggering. There's definitely a healthy dose of that!

Now, grab some Tootsie Pops, curl up in your favorite reading spot and enjoy the ride!

Much love,

Andi

This one is for my A to Z Books and More crew… Thank you for bringing me into the fold and supporting my work. It means more to me than I can say.

Meri...

Everyone knows me as Meri, the friendly bartender at Ballinger's, the local watering hole, but I have another name: Mistress Green. There aren't many who become acquainted with my alter ego, but those who do live to regret it.

My underground high-stakes poker games have earned me a lot of money in the two years since I've hosted them, but that all changes when my attraction to one of the participants gives the wrong impression to a few of the other players.

Poker swears he can protect me from any threat, but how is he going to do that when he's the reason I've become hunted in the first place?

Poker...

As the enforcer for the Soulless Kings MC, my world is dark and chaotic. I thrive in that darkness, but sometimes, even I need to experience some light. That's where Ballinger's comes in, and more specifically, Meri.

The alluring bartender has many qualities that captivate me, but when she becomes Mistress Green and hosts her poker games, all other women cease to exist. Our mutual desire is combustive, and it puts her life at risk in ways that make me crave death and destruction.

With the help of my club, I know I can protect her, but will she let me, or will her stubbornness cause me to lose her forever?

PROLOGUE
MERI

I'VE GOT A PLAN.

Two years ago…

"THIS CAN'T KEEP HAPPENING."

I smother the groan building at the back of my throat. I've been avoiding my landlord for days because I don't have the money for my rent, but the fucker caught up with me as I was leaving for work.

"I'll have it by next week," I tell him, praying like hell that I actually will.

Gerald sighs. "Meri, I've been more than patient with you since you moved in. But if I don't have that money in my hand by Friday, I'll have to start the eviction process."

"That's only three days!" I exclaim.

"And rent was due last week."

"I know, but—"

"But nothing, Meri," Gerald snaps. "Just pay your rent."

With that, he stalks away, back toward his own apartment, and I continue to my beat-up Camry. If I don't hurry, I'm going to be late for my shift at Ballinger's Bar. As the bartender, I make decent tips, but clearly not enough to keep my head above water.

"Glad you could make it," Grady, my boss and the owner of Ballinger's, quips when I stride through the bar's entrance.

"Sorry," I mutter. "Had a leak in my apartment, and the repairman showed up late."

Grady stares at me for a long moment before nodding. "Just text next time, ya?"

"Sure thing."

Grady is a decent guy, but I have no interest in sharing my personal problems with him. What I *am* interested in is finding a way to make some extra cash. I already work as many shifts as possible at the bar, so that's out of the question. But there has to be something I can do on the side.

As the night wears on, my mind races with possibilities, and every single time I'm able to slow down enough to really consider them, I keep coming back to one: poker games.

When I was growing up, my father ran a few poker games out of our garage, and I know that's the only reason there was always food on the table and clothes on my back. My mother was a waste of space, so my dad did what he had to do.

The problem with his *business* was that it attracted some pretty unsavory people. Every game night, I was either sent to my room and told to lock the door or shipped off to stay with my grandmother. Those nights were a mixture of fun and fear, depending on where I spent my time.

"Hey, Meri!"

I whip around and grin at the biker sliding onto a stool. "Hey, Poker. What can I get ya?"

Poker was my very first customer when I started at Ballinger's, and I liked him immediately. When he's here, I know it's going to be an entertaining shift.

"Just a beer," he replies and then tacks on, "And an explanation as to why I had to call your name five fuckin' times before you heard me."

I roll my eyes. "I guess I'm just stuck in my head tonight," I say as I take the cap off and slide the beer bottle toward him. "Want it on your tab, or are you actually gonna pay tonight?"

"Tab's fine. I'll settle up when you finally agree to go out with me."

His smirk is flirty, and we do this song and dance all the time. If I wasn't so worried about all the other women who ride his cock—I've heard the stories—I just might take him up on it. But as it stands, he's not the type to commit, and I'm not the type to share.

"Might want to talk to Grady about that plan," I tell him. "I'm pretty sure he'd rather you pay."

Poker shrugs. "Grady and the club have an understanding. I ain't worried." He punctuates that with a wink.

And dammit if my panties don't start to melt.

Several of Poker's brothers trickle in throughout the rest of my shift, and I don't get a chance to talk to him much more. That's fine, though, because I've got other things to worry about.

Like how to make more money.

Again, I come back to the poker games. Surely, I could do something like that, even in a small town like Marble Falls, Texas. The problem is, I don't want to be like my dad. If I were to run poker games, I'd do it differently.

"Last call!" Grady shouts sometime later.

By the time I'm heading home, my feet are killing me, but I'm not as worried about my future as I was earlier.

POKER

I've got a plan.

CHAPTER 1
POKER

I DON'T HAVE ANYTHING TO STOP ME FROM GOING DOWN THAT RABBIT HOLE OF FANTASY.

Present day...

"Hey, baby."

I frown at Kitty, the Bangin' Betty who currently has her hand down the front of my pants. When she was walking toward me, I tried to avert my eyes, but she doesn't know how to take a hint. I grab her by the wrist and yank her hand free of my jeans.

"Not interested," I snarl.

She stares up at me from beneath her fake eyelashes and pouts. "Since when, baby?"

Good question.

"Does it matter?" I counter, my brow arched dangerously high.

Sensing my annoyance, Kitty slowly backs away with her hands up. "Yeah, yeah, okay. But don't come cryin' to me later when your balls are blue."

With that, she spins on her heel and stalks toward the corner where several of my brothers are shooting the shit. That's the thing with Kitty... She doesn't give a rat's ass whose dick she rides, as long as the owner of said dick has a patch.

Soulless King MC patches might as well be a pussy magnet, they work so well.

"You feeling okay?"

I glance over my shoulder to see Screamer staring at me like I've got two heads.

"Yeah, why?"

His eyes dart across the room to Kitty before settling back on me. "I don't remember the last time you turned down that cunt," he says.

I shrug. "Like I told her, not interested." Bring my beer bottle to my lips, I ignore the warmth of the liquid and down the remainder in one long gulp.

"Since when?" my brother asks.

Slamming the empty bottle onto the bar, I wave at Jimmy, the prospect bartending at the clubhouse tonight, signaling him to get me another.

"Jesus, what do you care?"

"Don't care," Screamer states. "But it's weird, and I don't like weird."

"I'm fine, brother," I say with a sigh. "Just not in the mood to fuck is all."

"Would this have anything to do with a certain bitch in a green dress?" he asks, knowing me too fucking well for his own good.

My cock hardens painfully as an image of the woman in the green dress invades my mind. Her sultry brown eyes and long chestnut hair, coupled with the makeup she only wears during her game nights, are sexy as fuck, but those aren't the things about her that's ruined me for any other chick.

It's the way she handles the customers at Ballinger's Bar when they get a little too rowdy, and the way she flirts for bigger tips. It's the smile she's always wearing when I walk into the bar and her natural beauty that have dug their claws into my dick and won't let go.

Shaking my head, I flip Screamer off. "If it had anything to do with her, don't you think I'd be at Ballinger's instead of here?"

He grins. "Considering you've got a *guest* coming for the Nightmare Room, no, I don't."

At the reminder of the scumbag currently being transported to the clubhouse, I cracked my knuckles. As the club's enforcer, the Nightmare Room is like a second home to me. It's where I feel most comfortable.

Well, there and a certain abandoned warehouse.

I push away from the bar and stalk toward the door that will lead me to the stairs. Screamer practically cackles behind me, but I tune him out.

When I reach the lowest level of the clubhouse, the motion-activated lights flicker on as I walk down the hall toward the steel door to the Nightmare Room. I press my hand to the biometric lock, and the door slides open. As soon as I step into the space, my thoughts quiet, and my tense muscles loosen.

Taking my time, I gather weapons from the wall and set them out on the table below. I ensure that the meat hooks and chains attached to the ceiling are secure, and then, I wait.

It isn't long until I hear the sound of a body being dragged down the hall toward the room I occupy. My blood sings at the noise, and any thoughts of another place, a certain woman, disappear.

"Dammit, he's out cold," I snap when Ghost and Jackyl stride through the doorway with the elementary school principal.

"But alive," Jackyl retorts with a smirk.

A growl climbs up my throat, and I swallow it down. The fucker's right, but that doesn't mean I have to like it.

I watch as my brothers drape the man's bound wrists over the hook, and when they let go of his body, he jerks awake at the pain of his shoulders popping. He whips his head around, taking in his surroundings, and I know the exact moment he realizes he's fucked because his eyes widen and spark with fear.

"Where am I?" he demands, his voice steadier than I expect.

I tilt my head. "Does it matter?" Ghost and Jackyl back out of the room, and as soon as the door clicks shut, I advance on the man. "Cat got your tongue?"

"N-no, it d-doesn't m-matter," he stutters.

Grinning, I lift the serrated knife I'm holding and press the point into his crotch. He tries to distance himself but fails because of his restraints.

"Mr. Gromley, do you like your job?" I ask, circling his swaying body. "Do you think you're good at your job?"

"I-I don't k-know what you w-want me to s-say."

"Answer the questions," I sneer.

He swallows, his Adam's Apple bobbing, and I swear I hear it thunk.

"Love the job," he spits out.

"But you love the access it grants you to the kiddos more, isn't that right?"

His nostrils flare at the reminder of his extracurricular activities, and I have to swallow the bile that climbs up the back of my throat, knowing that the mere thought of said activities is turning him on.

Anyone who gets their jollies from little kids is sick and twisted and deserving of a one-way ticket to Hell.

"I d-don't know what y-you're talking a-about," he lies.

"Wrong thing to say," I snarl just before shifting my knife and plunging it into his gut, reveling in the way the life seeps from his gaze.

I could've drawn this out, savored his pain and made him suffer, but sometimes, quick is necessary. Taking my cell out of my cut, I shoot off a text to Jimmy, ordering him to come clean up.

As soon as I exit the room, my thoughts return to *her*, and I don't have anything to stop me from going down that rabbit hole of fantasy.

CHAPTER 2
MERI

Shit, he looks sexy in a tux.

"Can I get another Bud Light?"

I smile at Vince, one of the regulars at the bar, as I reach into the cooler and grab him his third bottle of the night. The second I set it in front of him, he lifts it to his lips and takes a long pull.

"I'll put it on your tab," I tell him with a smirk.

"You're a doll."

Rolling my eyes, I wipe down the bar, collecting recently left tips as I go. Tuesdays are notoriously slow, which is part of the reason I chose it for my other job. It's only a little after six, and I've got an hour to go before I can go home and change, but the game won't start until nine.

Plenty of time to mentally switch gears.

I picture the dress I set out before leaving for my shift, knowing I picked it because tonight a certain someone RSVP'd to my invitation to join the poker game I host. The emerald green satin flatters my curves, has an impossibly high slit up the leg, and a deep V that dips between my breasts to my belly button.

When I received the RSVP text on my burner, I almost swallowed my tongue. Poker comes to the games a lot, but this is the first time he's included the plus one I allow each player.

It's been two years since I started my side-venture of hosting high-stakes poker games. In the beginning, I would let pretty much anyone who could afford the ten-thousand dollar buy-in participate. That's no longer the case, and I'm much more selective. Only those who receive an invitation and RSVP can join, and I have enough players that they don't all get invited to every game. The dress code is black-tie, which I enforce, but typically, no one balks at that because they're all rich as fuck assholes.

I do allow a plus-one, but the additional guest is not permitted to play the game. All participants must surrender their cell phones and any other electronics or weapons at the door, or they're not permitted entry.

The only person who knows about any of this,

outside of my thoroughly vetted security and the players, is Poker. And he's the only person who has ever gotten a pass on my rules.

But tonight, because I sent an official invite, he's required to abide by the same protocols as everyone else.

And he's bringing a plus one.

"Earth to Meri!"

I whirl around, startled by Grady shouting my name. "Fuck, you scared me," I accuse.

"Sorry, but your shift was over ten minutes ago," my boss says with a smirk.

"Shit," I mutter, tossing my rag into the sink. After clocking out on the computer, I grin at Grady. "I'm out. See ya Thursday."

I always take Wednesdays off because I never know when the poker games will end, having learned that the hard way the first time it lasted until six in the fucking morning.

"Have a good night," he says to my back as I move through the doors that lead to the break room.

Twenty minutes later, I'm climbing into the shower to wash the bar stink off me. It didn't take long for me to make enough money to catch up on my rent and buy myself out of my lease, and a few months later, I was able to buy my current house.

It's nothing special on the outside, just a brick

ranch house with a few acres of property. The inside wasn't anything to write home about either, but I've had a lot of renovations done, and everything is perfectly me.

After drying my hair and doing my makeup, I slip into my dress and glance at myself in the full-length mirror. I've never considered myself vain, but damn, I look good. *Better than good.*

As I make my way into the two-car garage, I grab my Sig Sauer P365 and secure it in the holster at my thigh, completing my transition from Meri to Mistress Green. I might make the players forfeit their weapons, but I'm not about to be a sitting duck.

Climbing into my nori green pearl Lexus LC 500 convertible, I smile when I remember how I came up with my alter ego. It wasn't hard. Hell, it's probably too juvenile for the air of sophistication I wanted to portray, but I chose Mistress Green because green is the color of money.

And shit, do I have a lot of it now.

It takes less than ten minutes to arrive at the warehouse, and when I pull into the lot, I spot my head of security standing by the door. Conrad is ex-military, built like a tank, and as loyal as they come. He's been with me for a year and a half now, and I couldn't ask for someone better to have my back.

"Hey, Meri," he says with a smile when I reach

him. He and my team are the only ones who get to use my real name here. "Already have four players inside and waiting on three more."

"Thanks," I reply. "Anything I need to know?"

He shakes his head. "Nope. Tonight seems to be a pretty tame crowd." He shrugs. "Unless you count the way Mr. Neero was groping his wife while I was checking their IDs."

"At least it's Mrs. Neero and not his mistress again," I say with a chuckle. "That bitch is dumb as a box of rocks."

Conrad throws his head back and laughs. "Remember when she asked Mr. Neero why he was collecting twos when they're the lowest amount of points?" He guffaws. "Holy shit, the look on the man's face was priceless. I thought he was gonna kill her right then and there."

"Poor guy. He was trying so hard to bluff so the others would fold. He was a hundred grand in on that hand and had to quit after that."

"I wonder how he explained it to the missus?" he asks.

I lift my hands. "Don't know, don't care. What happens outside of the games has nothing to do with me."

He nods before his eyes dart to the entrance of the lot where headlights signal another arrival. "Well, better get back to it. Solomon, Grant, and Malcolm are inside."

"Thanks," I say when he opens the door for me. "See ya after."

Conrad winks. If he weren't happily married with two kids, and I weren't crushing on someone else, I'd totally shoot my shot with him.

When I step into the main area of the warehouse, I grin at the sight. What started as a dirty concrete space has been converted into a sleek space that reeks of money and power.

"Mistress Green, good evening."

I roll my eyes before pasting a smile on my lips and facing Ms. Graven. "Good evening, Bernadette. I'm so glad you could make it."

"Well, someone has to give these gents a run for their money."

Bernadette Graven is middle-age, stunningly beautiful, and as corrupt as they come. Fortunately, she doesn't live in or anywhere near Marble Falls. She's one of the numerous players who only join the game when they're in Texas on business.

"Yes, they do," I agree. "If you'll excuse me, I need to check in with my team."

Before she can respond, I hurry toward the self-serving bar where Grant is stationed.

"Lucky you," he jests. "She was the first to arrive and cornered me for twenty minutes."

My lips twitch. "I'm sorry."

"No, you're not," Grant says with a chuckle. "But that's okay. Now I'm real knowledgeable about the movers and shakers of Atlanta."

"Jesus," I mutter. "Isn't participating in my game enough to prove she's right?"

"Guess not."

I open my mouth to respond, but the entrance opening catches my attention. Sliding my glance that way, my throat goes dry.

Poker crosses the threshold, and a slim arm is threaded through his, but I can't see the owner of the offending appendage as they're tucked behind him to enter.

Shit, he looks sexy in a tux.

As the pair fully walk into the space, jealousy winds through me as my gaze travels from his plus one's stilettos, up her gorgeous legs, and then higher to her tight black spaghetti strap dress. And when my eyes land on her face, my heart stops.

Why the fuck would he bring a cop here?

CHAPTER 3
POKER

What gives is I'm... fucked.

"She looks pissed."

I glance at Addison, my president's old lady, and scowl. When she overheard me telling Crow I was coming to the game tonight, she begged to be my plus one. I was suspicious of her motives, seeing as she's law enforcement, but she assured me that her interest was mere curiosity and not work-related. It took Crow ordering me to take her for me to finally agree.

"I told ya this was a bad idea," I snap.

Addison smacks my arm. "Leave it to me, big guy. I'll fix this."

Before I can stop her, she pulls her arm free and

strides toward Meri. I swallow my groan and follow, my eyes never leaving Meri's face. The second I stepped inside, I caught sight of her and almost swallowed my tongue. The dress she's wearing sends every ounce of my blood to my cock, and it throbs behind these awful tuxedo pants.

As delectable as she looks, her eyes sparked with rage the moment she saw Addison.

"...cause any trouble."

I catch the tail end of Addison's sentence when I join them, still not avoiding the heat in Meri's gaze.

"Can I speak to you a moment?" Meri asks, the words clipped. She doesn't give me a chance to respond before grabbing my elbow and dragging me across the space toward a corner. "What the fuck were you thinking bringing her here?"

Bringing my hands to her shoulders, I give them a gentle squeeze. "Calm down, Meri. Addison isn't here as a cop. I promise."

She shrugs free of my grip, and I immediately miss her smooth skin. "Calm down? Jesus, Poker, you know who my players are. What do you think's gonna happen when they find out who she is?" I open my mouth to reply, but she rushes on. "And it's Mistress Green here, you know that."

The corners of my mouth tug up into a grin. "Yes, Mistress."

The tension leaves her body, and she exhales as her lips twitch. "You're impossible."

"Nah, just mildly annoying."

She waves her hand dismissively. "Stop trying to make me forget why I'm mad."

Realizing that she's truly panicked about the reactions of the others, I soften my expression. "Look, if I thought for a second that her being here was a danger to your reputation and what you've built, she wouldn't be here. I promise you that. Addison might be…" I glance over my shoulder to make sure we're not within earshot of anyone. "…law enforcement, but tonight, she's the old lady of a one-percenter motorcycle club president. Nothing more, nothing less."

"Lemme guess," she counters. "Crow didn't give you a choice but to bring her."

I shrug. "You know he can't deny her anything."

Ballinger's Bar might not be where the brothers always party, but we're not strangers either. Meri knows the guys, and they know her. She's comfortable with all of them, and that's only a part of her immense appeal.

"Yeah, yeah. Asshole lives and breathes for her."

"Exactly."

"Fine, but if anyone seems to suspect anything or if anything feels off, she's gotta go."

"Understood." I turn to walk toward the round table where the other players wait. "But nothing will happen. I promise."

Fortunately, Addison's presence doesn't raise any questions. Most of those in attendance tonight are from out of town and have no clue who she is.

Halfway through the game, my chips run out. I've been too focused on Meri—excuse me, Mistress Green—and the expanse of leg showing from the almost hip-high slit in her dress.

"What's up with you tonight, Poker?" Mr. Neero asks. "You usually give me a run for my money."

I narrow my eyes at him. Mr. Neero is a man who earned his money on the backs of those less fortunate, and I hate him. Taking his money has always brought me great satisfaction, especially when I know what I do with it.

"Just a little preoccupied, that's all," I respond coolly.

"Leave the poor man alone, Dan," Mrs. Neero says, sliding her hands over her husband's chest. "Can't you see he's smitten?"

Addison chokes on her vodka soda from her position standing behind me. "Oh, no, we're just friends."

Mrs. Neero smiles, flashing her too-white store-bought teeth. "Wasn't talking about you, honey."

"Actually, I am smitten," I say, earning curious

looks from everyone. "Smitten with money, and since I don't seem to be winning any, I'm out." I rise from my chair. "Mistress Green, always a pleasure."

I grip Addison's arm and lead her toward the exit. She doesn't say a word until we're in the matte black Camaro.

"Um, what the fuck was that?" she demands as I fire up the engine.

"What?"

"What was that bitch seeing that I wasn't?"

"What are you talking about?" I demand, harsher than I intend, as I peel out of the lot.

"Poker, no one could ever accuse you of being smitten." Addison laughs, and it grates on my nerves. "And that bullshit about money? C'mon, what gives?"

What gives is I was caught staring at Mistress Green and imagining her legs wrapped around my hips with that damn dress wrapped around hers. What gives is I like the woman and torture myself by going to the poker games just to spend more time with her and make sure she's okay. What gives is I'm... fucked.

None of those words come out of my mouth as I shrug. "Nothing gives, Addi. Just not a fan of the Neeros."

"I call bullshit."

"Call it whatever you want. I call it the fucking truth."

CHAPTER 4
MERI

Everything's great.

The bar is packed, keeping me physically busy, but mentally, I'm somewhere else. This week's poker game was a shitshow. Not only were there two no-shows, but the Neeros made Poker so uncomfortable that he left.

Unwanted and unwarranted jealousy spikes at the image of him walking out of the warehouse with Addison on his arm. There is less than nothing between them other than friendship. Does he love her? Absolutely. But not like that.

So why the fuck does the sight of them together make me feel like this?

"Do anything fun on your day off?" Lance, the other bartender, asks when there's a brief lull.

"Yeah, if you consider sleep fun."

His nostrils flare, and it's all I can do not to roll my eyes. Lance has hinted several times at the fact that he wants in my bed—not to sleep, by the way—but I'm not interested. Not only is he not my type, but he's a coworker.

I shudder at the thought.

"I wouldn't have let you sleep," he says, lowering his voice an octave.

Grabbing a rag from the sink, I wring it out and start wiping down the bar. "Was it busy last night?" I ask, changing the subject.

He chuckles. "One of these days, Meri, you're go—"

"Don't, Lance," I snap, throwing the rag at his chest. "Don't do this."

Lifting his hands, he backs away with a grin. "Understood."

When he disappears into the kitchen, I heave a sigh. Why is it that men think they can say anything they want to a woman, come on to them regardless of the number of times they've been told no?

I bend to grab the rag that fell to the floor, and when I straighten, Poker is sitting at the bar with a large grin on his face.

"If I'd have known that's the sight that was gonna greet me, I'd have come in earlier," he teases.

"Don't start," I snap, and guilt flashes in his eyes, causing my shoulders to sag. "Sorry."

"You know I didn't mean anything by that comment, right?"

I huff out a laugh. "Yeah, I know. You're about the only man who can get away with talking to me like that."

The guilt morphs to something else, something unidentifiable. "Other men talk to you like that?"

"Careful, Poker," I taunt. "Someone might think you're jealous."

He scoffs at that. "Nah. Just looking out for you is all."

Damn.

"I can take care of myself," I remind him.

"Never said you couldn't."

This time, I let the eye roll happen. "Whatever. What can I get ya to drink?"

"Surprise me."

I shake my head. "Okay."

A minute later, I set a cocktail glass with pink booze in front of him. "What the fuck is that?"

"Cosmopolitan," I reply, failing miserably to stifle my mirth.

"It's pink!"

"It is."

"What am I supposed to do with a pink drink?"

"Drink it."

"But… I…" He shakes his head as he sputters. "I can't drink that."

I tilt my head. "Why not?"

"It's pink," he repeats.

"Afraid it'll make your balls shrivel or something?"

"Or something," he grumbles.

"Just try it," I urge with a shrug. "Might even like it."

He mumbles under his breath before lifting the glass to his nose and sniffing. "Fuck, it even smells pink."

"Quit bein' a baby," I grouse.

Poker narrows his eyes at me, and with his gaze locked on mine over the rim of the glass, he pours it down his throat in one long gulp.

"Well?" I ask when he swallows and sits back. "Whaddya think?"

"It's pink."

I grin. "You said that already."

"It's not terrible," he admits. "And if you tell anyone I said that, I'll spank your ass."

Heat pools between my thighs, and I rub them together to ease the ache. "Like I'd let you anywhere near my ass."

He arches a brow. "You wo—"

"Yo, Meri, you've got a delivery."

The moment between Poker and me is ruined by Lance's statement. I was so caught up in the flirtatious exchange that I missed him returning behind the bar.

"What?" I ask.

Lance nods to his right, and that's when I see a man standing with a bouquet of roses in his hand.

"Are you M. Green?" the man asks.

I bristle at the use of Green as my surname. Only those who participate in my games know that name, but none of them know anything about my personal life, my real life.

"I thought your last name was Burns," Lance comments, his forehead creased.

"Green's my middle name," I blurt, and Poker smothers a laugh.

"Seriously?" Lance scoffs. "Your parents must've hated you."

Poker stiffens, turning his attention to the other man. "Watch it," he snarls.

"Uh, M. Green?" the delivery guy questions.

"Yeah, um, that's me," I tell him, taking the bouquet he hands me.

"Have a good night," he says before turning on his heel and walking out of the bar.

I glance from the flowers to Lance to Poker. The

latter is watching me intently, like he'll jump out of his skin if I don't tell him who they're from.

So not him.

I pull out the little card as I force my breathing to even out. This has to be a coincidence, right? Maybe they're from Addison for letting her stay the other night. She heard Poker calling me Mistress Green, so she assumed that's my actual name.

Yeah, that's what this is.

> *Thank you for an entertaining evening.*
> *-A*

Relief courses through me. I was right, they're from Addison. I make a mental note to thank her the next time she's in here.

"Everything okay?" Poker asks when the silence stretches.

I smile at him. "Everything's great."

CHAPTER 5
POKER

My brain is flooded with images of a woman in a sleek green dress.

"Fuck, this makes me feel old."

I smirk at Journey, who's sitting in the booth across from me at the only restaurant in this stupid town. We've been here for a little over an hour, surveilling the pricks across the street. Normally, we wouldn't give two shits about low-level dealers slinging their shit two hours from Marble Falls, but we got word that they're using our brand on whatever it is they're peddling.

And if I'm being honest with myself, the distraction is exactly what I need. Ever since Meri got those damn flowers the other night, I can't get her out of my head.

Not that you ever can.

"The second you let yourself get tied down," Python begins. "You got old. Might as well be a fuckin' grandpa."

Journey elbows him in the gut right as he takes a sip of his Coke, and Python scrunches his face at the burn from it coming out his nose.

"They can't be more than fifteen," Screamer comments, staring at the scrawny idiots who think they're being sneaky by sticking to a recessed entry of an abandoned storefront.

"The info Tracer got says they're mid-twenties," I remind my brothers. "Stop thinking of them as kids."

A blacked-out Escalade pulls up to the curb in front of the boys—let's face it, that's what they are—and I nod in their direction to get the others to look.

"The boss?" Python asks.

"Has to be," Journey concurs.

"Well, VP, what'll it be?" I query. "Can't exactly confront them in broad daylight."

"You and Screamer tail the SUV," our VP replies, his tone hard. "Python and I will stay here and keep an eye on the other two."

"You got it."

I toss a twenty on the table to contribute to the bill before Python and I make our way outside to our bikes. It's not like we have stealth on our side, so we don't bother to hide the fact that we're following the Escalade as we trail it out of town.

Fifteen miles after clearing the town limits, the vehicle turns off the main road and eases off to the side. I go around to the front while Python stays at the back, and both of us climb off our Harleys, guns drawn.

The driver's side window in the back slides down. "What's the meaning of this?" the man demands, his voice heavy with a Spanish accent.

"Who are you?" Python demands.

"The better question is," he drawls. "What the fuck you're doing on my turf?"

"Wouldn't need to be on your turf if you sold your own shit," I bark.

The door opens, and the man steps out. My eyes slide from his snakeskin boots to his expensive suit to his slicked back hair. He's young, maybe thirty, and he exudes power.

"Gentlemen, lower your weapons," he commands. His tone brooks no argument, and I find myself listening. Since I outrank him, Python follows my lead. "Now, let's talk like grown men, and I'm sure we can sort this out."

I may have lowered my gun, but my grip is still solid, and I'm still poised to take him out if necessary. "I'm Poker, and that's Python," I say, nodding at my brother. "We got intel that your dealers have been selling shit with the Soulless Kings MC brand on it."

The man dips his head. "Ah, yes, I have heard of the Soulless Kings. Ruthless motherfuckers, I'm told," he says with a grin that tells me he means it as a compliment. "I'm Esteban. I can assure you, I have no interest in utilizing any brand other than my own. If what you say is true, I will handle it."

Python laughs. "And we should trust you because?"

Esteban slowly swivels his head to stare at him. "Because I am a man of my word."

"And I'm fucking Santa Claus," I counter, firing my weapon at his feet, gravel spraying at the impact. "Ho, ho, ho, asshole."

Seemingly undisturbed, Esteban tilts his head. "That was unnecessary. If there's something you want, simply ask. I'm a fairly accommodating man."

"You can do what you need to do to handle your own crew, but we'll be there to make sure it gets done," I state.

He takes a deep breath, then another, and I start to think he's not going to agree, but then he nods. "That's fair." He moves to return to the back seat of the Escalade. "Meet me at the old Crane building at nine tonight."

With that, he closes the door behind him, and his

driver peels away, leaving Python and me in a cloud of dust.

"We're just gonna let him go?" Python snaps. "And where the fuck is the old Crane building?"

"Tracer can figure that out for us," I say, referring to our tech guy. "And yeah, we're letting him go. Journey and Screamer are still on the dealers, so if Esteban doesn't live up to his end, then we'll handle things ourselves."

Fortunately, later that night, Esteban *does* hold up his end of the deal. His dealers are taken out, and we're given assurances that our brand will never be on his product again.

As soon as club business is handled, the four of us make our way back to Marble Falls, and the entire way, my brain is flooded with images of a woman in a sleek green dress.

CHAPTER 6
MERI

Being Mistress Green gives me confidence and bone-deep knowledge that I can handle myself.

"I fold."

Poker tosses his cards onto the table before leaning back in his chair. He showed up at the warehouse on his Harley, wearing jeans, a dark Henley, and his cut. And while he was stunning in a tux, he's mouth-watering in his normal attire.

Tattoos cover his arms and are visible where he has his sleeves shoved up to his elbows. The top two buttons of the Henley are open, and I want to trace my tongue along the ink there.

"Mistress?"

I whip my head toward Malcolm, who's standing

to my left, where he watches over the players and game. "What?"

He nods at the table as he leans close. "The hand is over," he whispers.

Shaking my head free of my thoughts and returning my attention to the game, I gather the cards.

Poker clears his throat. "So, how's business, Martin?" he asks the man to his right.

Martin is the head of the largest private cybersecurity firm in Austin, and not a fan of the biker. "I can afford to be here," he sneers, barely sparing Poker a glance. "More than I can say for you."

"He's got a point, Mistress," Mr. Neero agrees. He came alone tonight, which only serves to make his tongue sharper. "Hell, he couldn't even bother putting on decent—"

"That's enough!" I snap, moving my stare from one player to the next until I've taken in each one. "If you don't like the way I run *my* fucking games, you can see yourself out."

Malcolm bristles beside me, braced for whatever might come from my outburst. When no one speaks, Poker stands and leans his palms on the table.

"If anyone has a problem with *me*," he seethes. "Then take it up with *me*, not *her*."

The deadly tone of his words sends shivers down my spine, but not in a bad way. Poker is defending me, and that feels… good. I mean, I can take care of myself, but I appreciate the sentiment, nonetheless.

"No problem," Stefan states, leaning back in his chair. "If I'm being perfectly honest, I'm quite happy to watch the man no matter what he wears."

Stefan is gay and has made no bones about what he thinks of Poker. The way he stares at him when they're both in attendance is intense enough to make me feel like a third wheel in a non-existent relationship.

"Thanks," Poker says. "I think."

"I apologize, Mistress," Mr. Neero says, his tone clipped. "It is not my intention to cause trouble. It just seems like there may be more to Poker being here than for a simple poker game. Especially when he's the only player who gets away with breaking your rules."

I breathe deeply, knowing he's right while simultaneously not giving a damn. My game, my rules, my exceptions to make. And I'll be fucked if I'm going to let any of these rich bastards try to guilt me into changing the way I do things.

"As I said, if you have a problem with the way things are run, you know where the door is," I repeat.

"Now, either shut up so we can continue or leave. I don't give a fuck which you choose, but you've got five seconds to make up your mind before I make it up for you."

Silently counting in my head, I get to one, and disappointment slithers through me when Poker turns and walks to the exit and out the door. It's all I can do not to flinch when it slams behind him, echoing in the large space.

"I see the trash took itself out," Mr. Neero mutters, and my blood boils.

"Get out," I say, rage bleeding from my tone.

"Excuse me?" the man scoffs indignantly.

"You heard me," I snap. "Get. Out."

When he makes no effort to move, Malcolm shifts to stand behind him, ready to force him out if necessary.

"You can't be serious." Mr. Neero halfheartedly chuckles. "You're a rich woman because of me."

My brows hit my hairline almost as quickly as I reach beneath my dress and yank my gun out of the holster to point it at his head. I'm grateful that my arm isn't shaking from my barely controlled anger. I'd hate to put a bullet in the wrong person.

"Get. The. Fuck. Out."

"You heard her," Malcolm says.

Grant finally makes his way from the bar toward

the table, his hand on the weapon at his side. He doesn't say a word, instead acting like a silent predator coming upon his prey.

Mr. Neero shoves back from the table and rises to his feet, buttoning his Armani suit jacket as he does. His face is a mottled red, and if it were possible, I'm sure smoke would be billowing out of his ears.

"You haven't seen the last of me," he seethes.

"You're suspended for one month," I tell him, regretting my three-strikes rule. This is only Neero's second, so my hands are tied. "The next time you accept one of my invitations, I'd appreciate it if you only bring your money and not your judgment."

With narrow eyes, he spins on his heel and storms out of the warehouse. Grant follows him to make sure he leaves, although I know Conrad would ensure it from his position at the exit.

"Any other grievances before we continue?" I ask, willing my heartbeat to return to normal.

For a moment, it pounded against my ribs hard enough to crack my chest wide open. Not from fear but adrenaline. As much as I hate confrontation, being Mistress Green gives me confidence and bone-deep knowledge that I can handle myself.

When no one speaks, I gather the cards and put them in the automatic shuffler. The last two hours of the game pass without a hitch, and Stefan is the big winner of the night, walking out with over a hundred grand in his pocket. I leave with thirty thousand after giving my security team the ten thousand each I pay them for each game.

Not bad for a few hours of work.

CHAPTER 7
POKER

The hardest thing I've ever had to do is walk away from her.

"Why are you still here?"

Leaning against the building, I watch Conrad out of the corner of my eye. I'm sticking to the shadows, more comfortable in the dark than the light. It serves me well because as players filter out of the warehouse, they don't even notice I'm standing here.

"I need to talk to Meri," I say, easily falling back on her real name.

Conrad tenses. "Mistress Green," he snaps.

I huff out a laugh. "Cut the shit."

"You're not needed here."

"Maybe." I shrug. "But the only way I'm leaving is if *Mistress Green* demands it of me."

"I could make you if I wanted to," he counters, the threat clear.

Slowly, I lean down and slide the knife he missed out of my boot. Then, so fast he doesn't know what hit him, I press the blade to his throat.

"Sure about that?" I taunt.

Conrad's eyes widen, and if I didn't actually like the man, I'd really show him what I'm capable of.

"Fuck," he mutters.

"Don't worry. I won't tell her you missed it."

When I lower the knife, his shoulders deflate. "Thanks."

"So, how's the family?" I ask him conversationally.

"How do you know I have a family?" he asks, his eyes narrowing.

"Seriously? Did you think I wouldn't do my homework?"

"But…"

"But what?"

"Why?"

Again, I shrug. "I needed to know that Meri was safe, that whoever she hired to have her back would actually have her back and not stab her in it."

He's quiet for a minute, his stare assessing. "You like her."

"And you don't?" I counter.

"Not like that, no. I'm married… happily."

"Meri's good people, and she's running a business in Soulless Kings' territory. Chalk it up to protecting my club."

"Right."

Before I can respond, the door opens, and the woman in question steps out. "Any trouble with Neero when he left, Conrad?" she asks, not seeing me at first.

His entire demeanor relaxes. "No, ma'am."

She nods. "Good. Don't worry about cleaning up. I'll come by tomorrow and handle it. Go home to the wife and kids."

"Are you sure? I don't mind staying a little longer."

"She's sure," I say, startling Meri.

When she levels her gaze on me, a blush creeps up her chest, bright in the security light. "What are you still doing here?"

"I asked the same thing," Conrad mutters.

"Just wanted to make sure you were okay after Neero's little outburst."

Her expression softens. "Oh, well, thanks. I'm fine."

"Can we talk for a minute?" I ask.

"Sure."

I gently grab her wrist and lead her away from

Conrad. When I stop, I don't remove my hand, instead keeping light pressure on her pulse point, loving the way it leaps beneath my fingertips.

Careful, Poker.

"You, uh, wanted to talk about something," she says, almost breathlessly, when the silence stretches.

For a moment, I forget what I wanted to talk about. I've got Meri alone, sort of, and all I want to do is lean in and capture her lips in a bruising kiss. Forcing myself to release her and step back, I shove my hands in my pockets.

"Is me coming to the games a problem for you?"

"What? No."

"Are you sure because tonight seemed to suggest otherwise."

"Neero?" she asks, her lips pursing for a second. "He's a dick, but I can handle him." She waves her hand dismissively. "Besides, I suspended him for a month, and it's his second strike. He knows he's walking on thin ice."

Relief washes through me, knowing she doesn't want me to stop participating. Then it's replaced by another, more sinister thought.

"Thin ice won't stop a man like that."

"I know what I'm doing, Poker," she insists.

Deciding to back off, I nod and let it go. "So, are you hungry?" I ask.

"Starved, but I'm more exhausted than anything else."

Unable to resist, I brush a wayward strand of hair behind her ear. She shivers at the contract. "Then you should go home and get some sleep."

Meri swallows. "I… Yeah."

"I'll come by tomorrow to help you clean up."

"You don't have to do that."

"I know I don't." I shrug. "But I'll be here. Go get some sleep."

The hardest thing I've ever had to do is walk away from her. Meri is intoxicating and if I didn't, I was going to shove her against the wall, hike up her skirt, and fuck her like my life depends on it.

The ride to the clubhouse goes by in a blur. My mind races with what happened at the warehouse, with all the ways things could've played out differently. When I'm not dwelling on the what ifs, my brain conjures up images of all the things I want to do with Meri.

When I walk into the clubhouse, it's quiet, but Crow is sitting at the bar sipping a drink. I make my way to him and slip onto a stool.

"How was the game?" he asks.

"Shitty."

He turns to face me and arches a brow. As he

takes in my expression, he grins. "She's getting to you, isn't she?"

"What are you talking about?"

"Brother, it's obvious you like her. You spend more time at Ballinger's than you do here, you haven't fucked a Bangin' Betty in I don't know how long, and we've donated to so many charities since you started playing in her games that the good people of Marble Falls are going to start thinking we're saints instead of sinners."

"Shut up," I snap, but then I heave a sigh. "Meri's…"

"She's what?"

I take a deep breath, fully intending to answer his question, but the one word—everything—on the tip of my tongue isn't what comes out.

"Call church for the morning, would ya?"

CHAPTER 8
MERI

How is it that this man can make me laugh when I'm madder than I ever remember being?

"Someone must've really pissed you off."

My forehead wrinkles with confusion at the hardware store cashier's comment. "Excuse me?"

The teenager nods at the items he's scanning. "This might as well be a murder kit."

I take in what I'm purchasing: garbage bags, bleach, other cleaning products, zip ties, a shovel, gloves, a roll of thick black plastic, and cute rubber boots with polka dots on them.

Damn, he's right. This looks bad.

Chuckling, I shake my head. "You either listen to too many podcasts or watch too much Dateline." The boy grins sheepishly. "I've got a property that needs to be cleaned, and I'm putting in a garden at my house."

"And the zip ties?" he asks, his curiosity getting the best of him.

"For my tomato plants. Little suckers need to be attached to the stakes, so they'll grow right."

"Whatever you say," he retorts, clearly not convinced.

He gives me the total, and I pay with cash, which only furthers his suspicion, if his expression is any indication. Poor kid's probably going to be watching the news for any murders for a while, wondering when I'll strike.

"Have a great day!" he calls after me as I exit the store.

Shaking my head, a grin splits my face.

Fucking kids and their overactive imaginations.

"Meri?"

I stop in my tracks at the familiar voice and turn to my left. Poker strides toward me, glancing at the items in my cart as he advances.

"What're you doing here?" I ask.

"Apparently, the same thing you are," he says, nodding at my purchases.

"Buying a murder kit?" I quip.

He rears back. "What?"

I explode into laughter at the horror in his eyes.

When I can't get control of myself, he rests his hand on my shoulder.

"Are you okay?"

By sheer force of will, I compose myself and grin. "I'm good. But shit, you shoulda seen the look on your face."

Poker shakes his head. "So, not a murder kit?"

"No." I tell him the same thing I told the cashier, and the relief in his eyes is comical. "I was just about to head to the warehouse to start cleaning up."

"Right. Which leads me back to your original question. I was gonna pick up some supplies before going there myself."

"Well, no need to waste your money," I tell him. "I've got it covered. And really, you don't have to help me. It's not like there's a lot to do."

"I'll meet you there," he says, leaving no room for protest. "You hungry? I can grab some takeout and bring it with me." My stomach chooses that moment to growl, and he chuckles at the sound. "Guess that answers *that* question."

"I could go for some pizza," I say.

"Works for me. Any preference on toppings?"

"As long as there's lots of cheese and no anchovies, I'm good."

"Got it." He starts to walk backward. "Gimme

time to order and pick it up, and I'll meet you at the warehouse."

After agreeing, I walk the rest of the way to my Honda Civic, the car I use for everything other than attending my poker games, and toss my stuff into the trunk.

Twenty minutes later, I pull into the warehouse lot and park near the front entrance. I grab the cleaning supplies and carry them to the door, digging through my purse for my second set of keys as I do. When I lift my gaze, I frown.

Taped to the door is an envelope with 'Mistress Green' scrawled on the outside. I drop my bags to the ground and yank it free. When I open it and pull out the piece of paper, my frown deepens, rage simmering just beneath the surface.

Mistress Green-

It is with great displeasure that I pen this note. I hope, given time, you will realize that you put your trust in people far beneath you. What must a man do to gain your favor? So far, it seems the only requirement is being a thug with horrible taste in attire. I won't beg for your affection or attention, but know this... If you don't start making better choices in the company you keep, you will suffer.

-N

Crumbling the paper in my fist, I shove it and the envelope into the bag of supplies and unlock the door. I stride into the large main area of the building and dump everything onto the bar. Needing to distract myself, I get to work.

By the time Poker arrives fifteen minutes later, I'm a sweaty mess, and my hair is piled on top of my head in a messy bun. I've been mopping the floor meticulously from one side of the space to the other, and I'm only halfway done.

"Damn, you weren't kidding about cleaning," he quips as he sets the pizza box on the bar.

"Nope," I say, my tone clipped, focusing on an invisible spot on the floor.

Poker grabs a slice of pizza and walks toward me

as he takes a bite. "What's wrong?" he asks when he reaches my side. "Did something happen?"

I stop mopping and lean on the mop, huffing out a breath. "Nothing happened. I'm fine."

He stares at me a moment before nodding. "Okay. Why don't you take a quick break and eat while it's hot?"

The scent of melted cheese and tomato sauce hits me, sending my stomach into another round of rumbling. "Yeah, okay. Thanks."

He follows me to the bar where we both stand and eat silently. Once half the large pizza is gone, I close the box and take a deep breath.

"So, wanna try this again?" Poker asks.

I glance at him. "Try what again?"

"What's wrong?"

"Nothing," I reply automatically.

"Bullshit. Talk to me, Meri," he presses. "Because when I left you at the hardware store, you were in a great mood, and now…" He shrugs.

"It's nothing, Poker," I insist halfheartedly.

"Again, I call bullshit. C'mon, we're friends, right?" I nod. "So, talk to me."

Sensing that he's not going to let this go, I sigh and reach into the bag where I stuffed the crumbled letter.

"This was on the door when I got here," I say after handing it to him.

Poker smooths out the paper and scans the words, his eyes sparking fire by the time he's done. "What the fuck?"

"Neero must've been more pissed than I realized last night."

"I don't give a rat's ass about his feelings," he barks. "This is a threat, and I don't like it."

"Neither do I," I admit. "I'm so mad I could…"

He levels his gaze on me and smirks. "You could what? Put your murder kit to use?"

His remark has the intended effect, and I burst out laughing. How is it that this man can make me laugh when I'm madder than I ever remember being?

"Feel better?" he asks.

"A little," I say, pinching my thumb and forefinger together. "I just don't get it. He's been playing for over a year, and you've been here almost every game he's at. Why does he have a problem all of a sudden?"

"He's just jealous."

I scoff. "Of what?"

Poker smirks.

"Of the way you look at me when you think no one is watching."

CHAPTER 9
POKER

Meri is a confident woman, and I kinda love that I'm throwing her off balance.

Meri's pupils dilate, and she ducks her head. I know my comment is throwing her off balance, but I'd rather that than her anger. I've got enough of that surging through my veins for both of us.

At church this morning, I discussed Neero with the club. I'd already had Tracer dig into the other players' backgrounds, and none of them are squeaky clean. But Neero is another story. While I wouldn't have put him in the threat category, he's certainly got some questionable business practices.

His attitude last night changed my perspective. Meri has always garnered respect and held her ground, but I could tell he rattled her. And now she has this note signed 'N'. The only logical conclusion is that it's from Neero.

"And what way is that?" she asks, pulling me from my thoughts.

"Like you want to lick me like a lollipop," I deadpan.

Her eyes widen, and her cheeks infuse with color. "Well, that was… specific."

"Yet you don't deny it."

Meri holds my gaze for a beat and then turns away. "Poker, I don't know what I'm supposed to say to that," she says as she moves back toward the mop bucket.

I snag her by the wrist and force her to face me again. "Don't do that."

"Do what?"

"Pretend like there's nothing here."

What the fuck am I doing?

"We're friends."

"Yeah, we are."

"What do you want from me?"

It's a fairly simple question, but the answer is infinitely more complicated. I want so much from her that it eats me up inside. But I also started this flirting to distract myself from my anger, so I didn't scare her.

I drop her arm and thrust a hand through my

hair. "I want you to be honest with me," I settle on saying. "It's clear that that note rattled you, so why are you trying like hell to make me think otherwise?"

"Maybe I am rattled," she says. "But I'm a big girl, Poker. I can take care of myself."

"How many times do I have to tell you that I never thought you couldn't?" I snap, annoyed.

"I... What do you want from me?" she groans.

"I want you to let me be your friend. Talk to me when something is bothering you. Ask me for help if you need it. Just... let me in a little."

Let me take care of you, protect you, be whatever it is you need in a man.

"And how exactly would you help me with this situation?"

I arch a brow. "Babe, I'm a Soulless King. If someone is giving you shit or threatening you, I'd show them in horrific detail exactly why that's the dumbest thing they could do."

Meri swallows, but her nostrils flare. "You say that like I'm yours to protect."

It's on the tip of my tongue to tell her she is, but I wisely keep that to myself. "You're my friend. Enough said."

"Can we just drop it, please? I really want to finish up here and get home."

I heave a sigh. I'm being a pushy asshole, and I hate it. "Yeah, sure."

We spend the next hour in silence. Once Meri declares the state of the warehouse 'as clean as it's gonna get', I help her carry the trash to the dumpster out back. After she locks up, she turns away from the building to face me.

"Thanks for your help."

"No problem."

She stares at me for a long moment before taking a deep breath and blurting, "How do you feel about gardening?"

"Um…"

"Never mind," she mutters and tries to step around me.

Again, I grab her wrist, and the softness of her skin sends shockwaves straight to my cock. "Why do you ask?"

She lifts her eyes to mine. "I'm going to work on my garden when I get home and then I'm gonna make some spaghetti. I always make too much so…" Her unfinished question hangs in the air.

"Are you asking me if I want to come to your place?"

"I…" Meri squares her shoulders. "Yeah, I guess. But it's stupid. Of course, you don't like to garden.

And I'm sure you'd much rather have steak than spaghetti."

I grin at her nervousness. Meri is a confident woman, and I kinda love that I'm throwing her off balance.

"You're right about the steak," I admit. "How 'bout I grab a couple at the store and meet you at your place? We can garden, and then I'll grill out." I tilt my head. "You do have a grill, don't you?"

"Yes."

"Then it's settled."

She nods once. "Okay. I, um… Give me your phone."

I reach into my cut and grab it to hand to her.

"What's your passcode?" she asks.

"Six three seven four," I reply with zero hesitation.

She taps on the screen a few times. I move to stand and look over her shoulder. Watching her navigate to my contacts and enter her own information makes my heart beat double time.

"There," she says as she hands the cell back to me. "Now you've got my address."

"Right."

"I'm gonna head home, so I'll see you when you get there."

"Okay. Need anything else at the store while I'm there?"

I repeat, what the fuck am I doing?

"No, but thanks," she says with a smile.

"Okay. See ya soon."

I move around her toward my Harley.

"Poker?"

I stop and glance over my shoulder. "Yeah."

"I would lick you like a lollipop."

CHAPTER 10
MERI

He makes it sound so easy.

"Don't you dare."

My grin widens as I haul my arm back, my hand filled with dirt. Poker and I have been working on my garden for two hours, and it's been fun. Comfortable.

"Or what?" I taunt.

His eyes fill with mirth as he pushes to his feet. I watch as he walks to my back deck, takes off his cut, and hangs it over one of the patio chairs. When he returns to stand in front of me, he spreads his arms out at his sides.

That's all the invitation I need. I throw the dirt, hitting him square in the chest before falling backward to my ass and laughing.

"You're gonna regret that," he growls, but there's no anger in his words.

"I doubt that," I manage to push out through my laughter.

Before I know what's happening, a large hand clasps around my ankle and drags me across the yard, making me grateful I changed into a tank and shorts I don't care about.

"Are you gonna apologize?" he asks when he stops and lifts the nozzle of the hose from the ground to aim it at me.

"Why would I do a cra—"

Cold water hits me in the face, and I sputter.

"I told you that you'd regret it," he says. I open my mouth to speak, but nothing comes out as more water fills my mouth. "What's that? I can't understand you."

I launch myself at him, and he drops the hose to take my weight, and we fall to the ground. Landing on top of him, I shake my head to loosen water from my hair and get him wet.

Poker glares at me, but the twitch of his lips and the press of his hardening dick against my stomach betray the anger he's trying to convey. Despite the cold from being wet, heat pools in my core.

"What are you doing to me?" he rasps, bringing his hands to rest on my hips.

My eyes slide closed at the contact. "Same thing you're doing to me," I whisper.

His sharp inhale sounds deafening in the still of the evening. All five of my senses are kicked into high gear until the only things penetrating through the lust-filled haze are the smell of dirt, the sound of our heartbeats, the feel of his body, the taste of my own fear, and the sight of arousal in his eyes.

After seconds that feel like a lifetime, Poker clears his throat. "You gettin' hungry, babe?"

His words are like ice on my overheated veins. Scrambling off of him, I jump to my feet and do my best to ignore the way my nipples are threatening to cut through the cotton of my tank. Of their own accord, my eyes lower to his erection, and I lick my lips.

"Starving," I finally find the presence of mind to say.

"Fuck, Meri," he growls as he stands.

My stare darts to his face, and satisfaction rolls through me at the strain I see there.

He's just as affected as I am.

"Keep looking at me like that, and I'm going to kiss you," he snaps.

"Okay."

In a split second, Poker's mouth is fused to mine. At first, the kiss is light, but as moments tick by, he increases the pressure and slips his tongue between my lips. His hands slide up my sides, over my shoulders, to the back of my neck, where he holds me to him like any amount of space between us would be physically painful.

I don't know how long we melt into each other, but when he pulls away, I sway toward him, reluctant to let him go.

"Why'd you stop?" I ask when the silence becomes too much to handle.

"Because if I didn't, I'd be fucking you into the ground like my very existence depended on it," he says bluntly, adjusting himself.

A giggle escapes me, and I slap a hand to my mouth. Poker only smirks.

"I like your honesty," I tell him.

"And I like every damn thing about you," he retorts. After several deep breaths, he asks, "Ready for me to make the steaks?"

"Yeah." I run my gaze down the length of his body. "If you wanna grab a shower first, feel free. I can throw your clothes in the dryer real quick."

"That'd be great, thanks."

Five minutes later, he's set up in the bathroom with a clean towel, and the dryer is tumbling. As for me, I'm doing my best not to think about the fact that Poker is naked... in my house.

He emerges from the bathroom ten minutes later, a towel wrapped around his waist. I swallow my tongue when he stands at the threshold to the kitchen.

"Oh, um..."

I move past him to the laundry room for his clothes. They're not completely dry, but they'll have to do because I don't have anything that will fit his massive frame. Our fingers brush when I hand them over, and electricity zings through my body, making me shiver.

"Cold?" he asks, and all I can do is shake my head. "Go get a hot shower, and I'll get dinner going."

It's an order, and one I have no problem obeying. I scramble to my bedroom and then into the attached bath. It crosses my mind that I could've let him use this shower, but something about it felt too... forward.

I remain in the shower until the water starts to run cold. Unfortunately, not enough time has passed that I'm any less desperate for the man who has gotten under my skin, into my soul. I'm not sure there's enough time in eternity for that to be a possibility.

When I enter the kitchen, dressed in clean shorts and a black tank, Poker is grabbing silverware from the drawer.

"Smells good," I say quietly, not wanting to startle him.

He turns around and freezes. Nerves attack me from the inside out, and I avert my gaze.

"Don't do that," he growls. "Don't hide from me."

With the air trapped in my lungs, I lift my head and level my eyes on his. "I don't know what's happening here," I admit.

Poker shrugs. "Do we have to label it? Can't we just take it a day at a time and see what happens?"

I consider that, and there's only one problem with his request. "I don't want to lose you as a friend."

He sets the silverware on the counter and stalks toward me. Bending slightly, he cups my cheeks. "Then we make a promise that, no matter what, neither of us will let that happen."

He makes it sound so easy.

"It is easy," he says, making me realize I spoke my thought out loud. "I like you, you like me. Simple as."

I huff out a breath, but before I can argue, he presses a soft kiss to my lips.

"Now, I don't know about you, but that steak is screaming my name," he says, his tone light. "Let's eat."

And just like that, the tension disappears, and we spend the rest of the evening just enjoying one another's company.

CHAPTER 11
POKER

I'm fucking trying, Pres. I'm fucking trying.

"Any news on Esteban?"

Screamer and I exchange a glance at the mention of the man we faced off with a week ago. Even though he held up his end of the deal and dealt with those in his crew who were appropriating the club's brand, we decided to put Tracer on him to see what he could find out about his *business.*

Know thy enemy and all that.

"I had one of my contacts make a buy from his crew," Tracer begins. "While our brand wasn't being used, the one on this batch of powder isn't exactly good news." He tosses a baggie into the middle of the table, and Crow snatches it up. "It's a fairly new brand, but it links back to the cartel."

"You've gotta be kidding me," Journey snaps.

"It's bad enough we've gotta deal with low-level idiots, but the cartel?" Jackyl gripes. "How are we supposed to go up against that?"

"We're not," Crow says matter-of-factly. "As long as they keep our name out of their business, we don't have beef with them."

"Uh, Pres?" I interrupt.

"What?"

"Maybe it's time we start discussing whether an alliance with the cartel would be beneficial."

"You really want to be in bed with them?" Python asks incredulously.

"He wants to be in bed with Meri, but—"

"Don't you fucking dare finish that sentence," I snarl at Screamer. "And no, I don't want to be in bed with the cartel, but we'd be stupid not to at least consider the pros of an association with them."

"If we're gonna talk pros, we need to talk cons, too," Ghost adds. "Can't have one without the other."

"Maybe you could get Esteban into one of the poker games," Stunner, our treasurer, suggests. "You're always talking about how you can learn a lot about a man based on how they play cards."

Instantly, I bristle. "Not happening."

"Why?" Crow demands.

POKER

"I'm not about to put Meri in that position."

"Wait a sec," Ghost says. "You want the club to trust him, but you don't trust him with your girl? How the fuck does that make sense?"

My girl?

"Doesn't Meri have a security team?" Journey asks, not giving me a chance to lose my shit on Ghost.

"Yeah, she does, but—"

"And if you're there, she'll be safe," Screamer adds. "Besides, I'm with you. I don't think Esteban is a threat to her safety or ours. As long as we don't cross him, that is."

"All in favor of Poker asking Meri to let Esteban into the game, thump twice," Crow instructs, putting it to a vote.

I'm the only one who hesitates, but I pound the table twice when I see I'm outnumbered.

"That's settled then," Crow says and looks at me. "Talk to her as soon as you can."

"I will."

Pres focuses on Stunner. "Give us a quick financial rundown."

"Things are good across the board," he reports. "And we got a lovely fruit basket thanking us for our latest donation to the elementary school."

"A fruit basket?" Journey asks.

Stunner shrugs. "They also invited us to attend the little graduation ceremony for the fifth graders on Friday. Apparently, some of the money was used to ramp up the celebration."

"Jesus," Journey mutters.

"What'd you tell them?" Crow asks, trying like hell not to laugh at Journey's discomfort.

"I told them that we'd do our best to be there," Stunner admits. "Wasn't sure if you'd want me to commit to it or not."

"We'll be there," Crow says. "At least patched members and old ladies."

"I'd like to bring Meri," I blurt. When all eyes turn to me, my muscles bunch. "What? We're able to make a lot of these contributions because of the game she hosts. She deserves to see the good that comes of it."

"He's got a point," Screamer says, always having my back.

Crow sighs. "Fine. But I'm telling you now, brother… If you want her to attend club functions other than parties open to the public, you better lock it down."

"I'm working on it," I mutter.

"Work faster," Journey taunts.

I glare at my VP. "Right, because you, Crow, and

Ghost didn't have your women all up in our business before you *locked it down*."

"Enough!" Crow shouts. "This isn't up for debate. Not only does Meri associate with potential enemies, but you are way past liking her. Just do what you need to do."

"You kidnapped our enemy," I counter. "Or have you forgotten that Addison is a cop?"

"Keep my old lady out of this," he snarls.

I heave a sigh. "Yeah, fine."

"Anything else?" Crow asks. When no one speaks, he continues. "Church dismissed. And Poker, this is your one free pass. Bring Addi into shit again, and I'll feed you your dick."

Huffing out a laugh, I nod. "Got it, Pres."

My brothers file out of the room, but a hand lands on my shoulder before I can cross the threshold. I turn around to see Crow standing there with a grin.

"You know I'm only doing this because I see how much you like her, right?"

"Okay."

"You've had it bad for her since the first time you saw her. Do yourself, and the rest of us, a favor and claim her."

With that, he moves past me, leaving me alone with my thoughts.

I'm fucking trying, Pres. I'm fucking trying.

CHAPTER 12
MERI

I should be afraid of the darkness in his expression, but I'm only turned on.

"Is it a full moon or something?"

I laugh and shake my head at Grady. The bar has been packed since we opened, and we've had our fair share of asshole customers. The latest caused his question when she propped her giant fake tits on the bar and told him to reach into her cleavage for his tip.

"I wish," I say. "At least then we'd have an explanation for the insanity."

"What I wouldn't give to have a few of the Soulless Kings in here tonight," he comments. "At least when they're here, people try to keep their crazy to themselves a bit."

At the mention of the club, my stomach flip-flops. It's been a week since I've seen Poker, a week since that night at my house. I haven't stopped thinking about him or that kiss. I've been hoping he'd come to Ballinger's, but so far, he hasn't shown his face.

He has called me, though, but it was only to ask if I would send an invitation to one of the poker games to a man named Esteban. More specifically, he asked me to make it for the night that Mr. Neero would be permitted to return. I questioned him as to why, but all he said was something about being able to tell a lot about a person based on how they play cards.

Whatever that means.

Of course, I agreed. I'm learning that I'd do anything for Poker. Not because I feel like I have to or because he scares me into submission, but because I want to. I fucking like him, and it's messing with my brain.

"Speak of the devil," Grady says, pulling me out of my head, and I follow his gaze toward the entrance.

Poker's eyes immediately find me, and a smile tugs at the corners of his mouth. Smiling back, I track his movement as he stalks across the bar until he stops across from me.

"Hey," he says as he glances around. "Busy night."

"Hopefully, people will tuck their crazy away now that you're here," Grady says with a laugh.

"That bad?" Poker asks, a brow arched.

I grin. "It's been an interesting night."

"Yeah, if you think the fact that I'm going to have to burn this bar top after we close is interesting, sure, it's been interesting," my boss grumbles as he moves away from us to take care of customers at the other end of the counter.

"I don't think I've ever seen him so annoyed," Poker comments with a grin.

"Me either." I shrug. "So, what can I get ya?"

"Surprise me."

I smirk. "You sure you want me to do that after last time?"

He narrows his eyes. "How about a beer, and you can surprise me with a shot?"

"You got it."

I grab a bottle of his favorite brew from the cooler and uncap it before setting it in front of him. Then I go about making him a shot that I know he'll like. When I slide it across to him, he eyes it warily.

"What is it?"

"Just toss it back," I instruct. "Promise you'll like it."

He does as instructed, and his eyes light up.

"Damn, that is good. What's it called?" he asks as he lifts his beer to his lips.

I smirk. "Blowjob."

Poker chokes on his booze, coughing so hard his eyes water. "Fucking hell, babe," he says when he catches his breath.

"I'll have one of those."

Both Poker and I turn to face the man who just stepped up to the bar.

"You want a Blowjob?" I ask, not even realizing how that sounds until the guy opens his mouth again.

"You offering, sweet cheeks?"

Poker's eyes narrow to slits, and I can see his body vibrating with rage, but when he only stares at me and doesn't move, I realize he's giving me a chance to handle this before he does.

"I'm offering the drink, not the act," I tell the customer as I grab a clean shot glass from beneath the bar.

"Aw, c'mon, sweet cheeks," the guy cajoles as he grabs his junk. "You can take a big drink of my cu—"

The next thing I know, the guy's on his ass, and Poker's standing over him, his chest heaving. I lean across the bar to take in the man's face, and he's holding his nose as blood seeps from beneath his fingers.

"What the fuck, man?" he cries.

"The only cock going between her pretty lips is the one swinging between *my* legs," Poker seethes.

It's on the tip of my tongue to protest, but the fire that roars straight to my core keeps me from saying anything.

"Whatever," the guy huffs. "No bitch is worth this shit."

He tries to get to his feet, but Poker stomps a booted foot into his chest, slamming him backward. "Her name is Meri, not bitch. Now, get the fuck outta here before I decide you *are* worth the effort it takes to kill you."

Poker lifts his foot, and the man scrambles to his feet. Grady has made his way around the bar and escorts the prick out, ordering him never to show his face again.

"Meri is mine," Poker barks at no one in particular, and everyone within hearing distance. "Consider this a preview of what happens when my woman is disrespected."

It's quiet for a few seconds, but then the chatter starts back up like nothing happened. Poker turns to me, and I should be afraid of the darkness in his expression, but I'm only turned on.

"Your woman?" I ask.

"Got a problem with that?" he counters as he sits on his vacated stool.

Vigorously, I shake my head. "Nope."

"Good." Poker sips his beer while I take care of a few customers who, shocker, don't order Blowjobs. "Hey, do you work on Friday?" he asks when I return my attention to him.

"I don't think so, why?"

"I wanna take you somewhere."

"Where?"

He grins, and my panties melt. "It's a surprise."

I groan. "I'm not a huge fan of surprises."

"You'll like this one, I promise."

"And if I don't?"

"Consider it payback for getting me all hot and bothered in public," he states, lowering his hand to adjust himself.

CHAPTER 13
POKER

Just being near her is like standing in the presence of something all powerful.

"What the fuck are you smilin' at?"

I shake my head at Screamer as I read Meri's text.

> Meri: Since you won't tell me where we're going, can you at least tell me what to wear?

"It's gotta be Meri," my brother grumbles.

"Yep," I reply as I text her back.

> Poker: Your bday suit

> Meri: I'm serious 😠

> Poker: So am I 😇😈

> Meri: Poker, dammit

> Poker: Fine. Just something casual. We're taking my bike so boots and jeans for sure

> Meri: K

> Poker: See ya @ 4

The elementary graduation doesn't start until seven, but I want to take her to a few other places around town beforehand. Satisfied that our text exchange is over, I pocket my cell.

"Have you told her she's yours yet?" Screamer asks.

Rolling my eyes, I nod. "Yeah. Had to when I stupid fuck asked her for a blowjob at Ballinger's."

His brows shoot to his hairline. "Is he still breathing?"

"Unfortunately."

"How'd she handle that?"

"She was fine."

"So, the two of you are like a thing now?"

The question rattles in my brain for all of a second. "Yep."

"Good for you."

"Thanks, brother. Meri is…"

"Perfect for you," he says when I let the sentence hang.

"She really is."

Screamer slaps me on the back. "Now all ya gotta do is let all the Bangin' Betties know you're taken," he teases. "They're gonna love that."

I scoff. "It's not like I've fucked any of 'em recently."

"Doesn't matter, man, and you know it."

"Yeah, yeah." I stand from the couch in the common room. "I gotta get ready. I'll see ya later at the school."

"See ya."

An hour and a half later, I pull into Meri's driveway. As I dismount my bike, she steps out the front door, and my mouth goes dry.

Holy. Fucking. Shit.

How can this woman look so damn tempting in dark wash jeans, a form fitting green tee, and black leather jacket? I've seen her in dresses that expose far more skin, but she's equally, if not more, beautiful like this.

"Is this okay?" she asks when she reaches my side.

"Perfect," I groan before pulling her against my chest and capturing her lips.

Meri sighs into the kiss, licking her tongue into my mouth with so much passion I fear I might combust. Knowing that if I don't stop, we'll never leave her house, I reluctantly pull away but keep my hands at her hips.

"We should go," I tell her.

She nods, and I help her onto the back of my bike. Meri isn't hesitant, and as soon as I settle in front of her, she circles my waist with her arms. I navigate us out of her neighborhood before wrapping my hand around her thigh.

This feels right... me holding her, her holding me, both of us on my Harley.

When I reach our first destination, Meri climbs from behind me easily. She looks from the building to me.

"You in the market for a dog?" she asks.

"Nah."

I grab her hand and thread my fingers through hers. The move is automatic, like I've been doing it my whole life. We walk into the animal shelter and are greeted right away.

"Hey, Poker," Jinny says with familiarity.

Meri bristles next to me so I squeeze her hand.

"Hey, Jin. This is Meri, my girlfriend. Meri, this is Jin. She keeps things running smoothly here for the animals."

Meri instantly relaxes. "Nice to meet you."

"You, too," Jinny states. "You must be pretty incredible if you got this joker to settle down."

"She is," I confirm.

"So, what brings you by today?" Jinny asks. "We're still working through your last donation, so I know it's not to bring another."

"Donation?" Meri inquires.

"Yeah," Jinny confirms. "Poker and the club donate to the shelter regularly. And I can't tell you how much we appreciate it. Because of them, we have the means to operate a no-kill shelter and provide any and all necessary vet care. Our babies are fed, have toys, and we have actual staff along with volunteers, so the animals are never alone."

"Wow," Meri exclaims as she eyes me. "Does the club do fundraisers or something? Why haven't you told me about them?"

I shake my head. "No fundraisers. All our donations are possible thanks to a high-stakes poker game I play in sometimes," I explain, choosing my words carefully so I don't out Meri to Jinny.

She gasps. "That's... You never told me." Her tone is accusatory, like I lied to her or something.

"Wasn't trying to hide it," I assure her. "Just not doing it for recognition. Honestly, the only reason you know now is because I wanted you to see the good that you're making possible. And because I don't want there to be secrets between us." I glance past her to Jinny. "Can we see some of the dogs?"

Jinny grins. "Of course. I'll get some of them gathered outside in the exercise yard."

When she walks away, I pull Meri close. "Tell me what you're thinking." She hesitates, and I add, "Please."

"I'm..." Meri swallows. "I'm thinking that what started as a crush could easily turn into something serious."

"Is that a bad thing?"

"No, not bad, just..."

"Just what?"

"Isn't this a little fast?" she asks.

"Does that bother you?" I counter.

"No, but I figured it would bother you."

"Why would it bother me?"

She laughs, but there's no humor in it. "Because you're this badass biker who could have any woman he wants. Hell, I've seen you with beautiful women at the bar. I don't know why you want to settle for me."

Meri is not a woman who shows vulnerability. She always projects confidence, so her statement takes me by surprise.

"First, I don't want *any woman*. I want you," I tell

her honestly. "Second, any other female's beauty pales in comparison to yours, whether you're in one of your sexy green dresses or sweats or a flour sack. And third, I'm not settling. You're so far out of my league it's insane, but I'm not about to look a gift horse in the mouth." I give her a quick peck. "Now, wanna see some dogs?"

She nods with a small smile.

We hang out at the shelter until it's time to leave for the elementary school. I've spent the last hour and a half watching Meri's excitement with each new dog Jinny introduced her to, listening to her laughter at all the canine antics.

"Why do I have a feeling you'll be back to pick out a new fur baby?" I tease her as I help her onto my bike.

"Oh, I'm so coming back. Chaos, that Great Dane, was so damn cute. I need him in my life."

"He was pretty cute," I admit.

The ride to the elementary school only takes five minutes, and after parking, Meri looks at me with confusion.

"Uh, why are we at a school?"

"It's the fifth-grade graduation," I explain. "The club needs to show their support because we were invited due to our donation."

"More donations made possible by Mistress Green?" she asks.

"Exactly."

Meri smiles at me, and it's blinding in the most stunning way. "Thank you."

"For what?"

"Showing me this. It means a lot."

I shrug. "Better get used to it, babe. You're mine now which means you're a part of this world."

The rest of the evening goes by in a blur. Graduation goes off without a hitch, but I barely remember any of it because of the woman at my side. Just being near her is like standing in the presence of something all powerful. She's burrowed her way into my heart, and I'll be damned if I ever let her go.

It's a few hours later that I drop her off at her house.

"I had fun today," she says as I walk her to her door.

"Me too."

"Wanna come in for a bit?"

"Do I want to? Absofuckinglutely. But I can't."

Meri frowns. "Why not?"

"Club business."

"Oh. Okay."

I can tell she wants to ask questions, but she doesn't. "No secrets between us, right?" She nods. "I promise you I will never lie to you, but when it comes to club business, I don't have a choice as far as not discussing it. Don't think of it as secrets but more like government clearance. There are just some things people can't know."

She seems to think that over for a minute before replying. "Makes sense. And I don't expect you to betray your club. Your loyalty is one of the things I like about you. Just don't keep me in the dark about anything personal or that has to do with me, okay?"

"Promise."

I lean my forehead against hers, about to kiss her, but she startles.

"Oh, shit. I almost forgot. I got Esteban's RSVP for the game. He didn't add a plus one though."

"That's good," I tell her. "We need to talk about security for the game he's attending. I know you've got your team, but I'd really like for some of my brothers to be there as well."

"I…" Meri swallows. "Is it important?"

"It is."

"Is it necessary?"

"Yes."

"Is it because of club business?"

"Yes."

"Okay. I'll give Malcolm, Solomon, and Grant the

night off that week. But Conrad stays. That's not negotiable."

"I'm good with that. My brothers will be too." I kiss her quickly before I start to back away. "Thank you. Now, get inside and get some rest. I know you've got a long shift tomorrow."

"'Night, Poker."

"'Night, babe."

CHAPTER 14
MERI

No secrets.

"I call."

I watch as Martin tosses chips onto the middle of the table. Next to him, Ms. Rogers rolls her neck, which is her tell that she has a shitty hand. I don't know if the others have picked up on this, but I sure have. Behind her is Diego, the woman's plus-one for the night.

"Rogers," Stefan prods. "You in or out?"

The middle-aged socialite from California straightens her shoulders and reaches for her chips. "Call."

Stefan groans. "I fold."

After tossing his cards down, he rises from his

chair and makes his way to the bar. Diego's gaze follows his movement, but I remain focused on the game.

The rest of the hand plays out, and Martin wins. Ms. Rogers whines about the money she lost but seems to calm when Diego leans over and whispers something in her ear.

Poker isn't here tonight, though I wish he were. I'm frazzled since getting that note at my house from Neero. Granted, the guy's month isn't up yet so he's not here, but that doesn't seem to matter.

"Everything okay?" Martin asks me.

"Of course," I reply, smoothing my hands down the satin of my dress. "Why don't we take a few minutes before the next round?"

The players don't move away from the table, but I do. I walk across the large space to the small office I keep and kick off my shoes as soon as I enter. For some reason, my heart just isn't in the game tonight. I'd rather be with Poker.

Fuck, I miss him.

Make no mistake... It's only been twenty-four hours since I've seen him, but he's quickly become an integral part of my life.

I reach into my purse for my cell so I can send him a quick text.

POKER

> Meri: Wish you were here.

He doesn't respond, but I don't expect him to. He told me he had more club business to handle, and I trust that he's busy.

As I move to put my shoes back on, the door opens, and Diego strides in.

"You can't be in here," I snap, annoyed that he got past my security team.

Lifting his hands in mock surrender, he smiles, but it's not a nice smile. It's handsome, sure, but it's hard, brutal. "Just wanted to ask you a question," he says.

"What?"

Before I know what's happening, he lunges forward and pins me to the wall. "Where's your boy toy?" he sneers, his nose pressed to my cheek.

"Excuse me?"

"Don't play stupid bitch with me," he snarls. "That biker boy I've been told you eye-fuck on the regular… Where is he?"

"He's not here, obviously. What do you want with him?"

I want to ask how he knows about him, but I'm not an idiot. The players of this game might not interact on the daily, but I know they have some contact outside of these walls, despite being geographically separated. Ms. Rogers clearly told Diego about Poker, and no doubt she heard whisperings from the night Neero was suspended.

Fucking gossip.

"That's a shame." Diego licks my cheek, and I try to shove him away, but he's too strong. "I've got a message for you to deliver."

"Fuck you," I spit out.

"No thanks." He tilts his head, his arm still braced across my chest to hold me in place. "Now, you're gonna tell Poker that he and his club are to stay clear of my brother."

"Who's your brother?"

"Poker will know. Deliver the message."

Diego pushes away from me and storms out the door. It takes me a minute to regain my composure, but when I do, I return to the main area of the warehouse. I scan the space, but both Diego and Ms. Rogers are gone.

"You okay?" Malcolm asks when he reaches my side halfway to the table. "I saw Diego high-tail it from your office, and then the two of them took off."

I absently rub my fist against my chest. "I'm fine. Let's get these last two deals over with."

Malcolm silently escorts me back to the table, and

the remaining rounds go smoothly, but my mind stays on Diego and his message.

Who is his brother?

What is Poker and the club involved in?

Is Ms. Rogers connected or just a coincidence?

By the time the evening comes to an end, I'm mentally drained. Conrad and the guys begin to clean up while I grab my purse from my office and head to my Lexus. I'm not paying attention, my face buried in my cell, so when I run into a wall of muscle, I let out a scream.

"Meri, it's me!" Poker shouts, wrapping his arms around me.

His voice washes over me as I try to smack him but can't with the way he's got my arms trapped between us.

"Jesus, you scared the shit out of me."

"I'm sorry," he rumbles. "Wasn't going for that. I figured you'd see me."

Breathing deeply, I ease away from him. "You don't have to apologize. I wasn't paying attention."

He stares at me for a long moment as if assessing my demeanor. "You okay?"

"Yes." *No secrets.* "No," I say and shake my head. "Come back to my place tonight?"

"Wanna take my bike or your car?" he asks without hesitation.

"We can take both. I don't want to leave either behind. Just… follow me, okay?"

"Is everything okay?"

"We'll talk back at my place, I promise."

"Okay." He presses a kiss to the top of my head. "I'll be right behind you."

CHAPTER 15
POKER

AS LONG AS YOU HAVE ME, MINE IS THE ONLY TOUCH YOU SHOULD EVER EXPERIENCE.

SOMETHING IS WRONG.

Meri is rattled.

My woman screamed, and it was a scream of terror, not shock.

Before we reach her house, I vow to get to the bottom of it.

When we reach her house, I watch Meri carefully. She appears calmer as I follow her inside, and I breathe a sigh of relief. Make no mistake about it, there's still something wrong, but maybe it isn't as bad as I feared.

"Rough night?" I ask her.

"You could say that." She walks into the kitchen and opens the refrigerator. "Wanna beer?"

"Sure, thanks."

It takes her several minutes to make her way back to me in the living room, and as soon as she hands me the bottle, she flops onto the couch.

"I need to tell you something, and I know it's going to make you mad," Meri says quietly.

My heart skips a beat. "Okay, I'm listening."

"You know Ms. Rogers from the games?"

"Of course, I do."

"She brought a plus one tonight, a man named Diego."

"Good for her," I say with a chuckle. "Always did think she needed to get laid to dislodge that stick up her ass."

Unable to help herself, Meri laughs lightly. "Very true."

"So, this Diego guy," I remind her when she doesn't continue. "He do something?"

Slowly, as if she's dealing with fine China, Meri sets her beer on the coffee table before plucking mine from my grasp and doing the same. Then she turns and sits sideways so she's facing me.

"Before I tell you, I need you to take a good look at me and realize that I'm okay."

Instantly, my muscles tense, and my blood boils. "I'll fucking kill him," I snarl.

"Poker, I'm fine. He didn't..." She takes a deep breath. "He didn't hurt me, not really."

"What do you mean *not really?*"

Meri sighs. "He followed me into my office and pinned me against the wall." She slips the straps of her dress off her shoulders and tugs it down to reveal the swell of her breasts above the strapless bra she's wearing. "See, I don't even have a mark from it."

"He put his hands on you?"

"Technically, he put his forearm on me."

"Not helping," I snap.

Again, she sighs. "He said he just wanted me to give you a message."

I shoot to my feet and begin to pace. If he did this to get a message to me, then it's my fault that Meri was in danger. That thought sends my rage spiraling to an almost uncontrollable level.

"What's the message?" I ask her, my tone clipped.

"He said that you and the club need to stay away from his brother."

"Who's his brother?"

"No idea. He said you'd know who he is."

"What's Diego's last name?"

"Um..." Meri rises from the couch, holding her

dress in place with one arm, to retrieve her cell from her purse on the kitchen counter. After tapping on the screen a few times, she brings it to show me. "According to Ms. Rogers' RSVP, his full name is Diego Rivera."

"That means nothing to me," I admit.

"Maybe one of your brothers will recognize the name."

"Yeah, maybe."

My mind races with possibilities. It's not like the Soulless Kings don't have enemies. Hell, we collect them like some people collect stamps. But right now, things are good. No reports of enemies that are a current threat.

I need to call Crow, talk to all of them about this, but when I return my gaze to Meri, I realize the only thing I need to do at this very minute is take care of her and assure her that she's safe.

She might not be saying it, but she's not okay.

Grabbing her cell, I toss it onto the couch and then tug her against my chest. "You know I won't let anything happen to you, right?"

"I know."

"And I'll figure this out. Whoever this Diego and his brother are… they won't come near you."

"Okay."

I lean back and tip her chin up with my finger.

"What do you need from me? How can I help you salvage the night?"

Meri's pupils dilate, and her skin flushes. "Make me forget the feel of him," she whispers.

Diego may not have touched her intimately, but he still touched her, and that's a violation.

Bending, I lift Meri into my arms, and she wraps her arms around my neck. "Bedroom?" I rasp.

"Last door on the left."

I carry her to the room and upon entering, I immediately see she has an attached bath. "Shower first?"

"Yes, please."

I set her on her feet on the tile floor, and she strips while I adjust the water temperature. When I turn around and see her naked for the first time, I silently thank whatever deity is out there for making her mine.

"You are so fucking beautiful," I say reverently.

Meri blushes. "Thanks. I'd say the same, but you still have clothes on," she teases.

Quickly rectifying that situation, I strip and toss my clothes to the floor and move to stand a few inches away from her. Tentatively, she presses her palm to my chest, and my skin ripples at the contact.

I guide her into the shower, knowing if I let her

explore like she seems to want to, I'll be coming like a teenager who just discovered pussy. Meri stands under the spray, and I lean forward to press my lips to her collarbone. I trail kisses along her throat, making sure to erase the impression Diego may have left.

"Poker," she whispers, threading her fingers in my hair and pulling me closer.

Lowering to her nipple, I suck it between my lips while tweaking the other with a free hand.

"Oh God," she moans.

My cock is so hard I feel like it'd cut through glass like a hot knife through butter, but I focus on her pleasure. Easing her backward until she bumps against the wall, I drop to my knees.

"Hang on, babe," I growl, and that's the only warning I give her before burying my face in her pussy and lavishing her clit with my tongue.

Her legs tremble, so I wrap one arm around her thigh to help hold her steady as she grips my shoulders for support. Using my free hand, I drag it through her slit and groan at how wet she is for me.

"More, Poker," she pleads. "I need more."

Not one to deny her anything, I lick a path through her folds before shoving two fingers inside just as my tongue returns to her clit. Her knees threaten to buckle, so I tighten my hold.

I work my digits in and out of her, the rhythm of

my mouth and hand in sync, until she's a sexy, quivering mess. Her walls begin to spasm, holding my fingers hostage, and I hum against her flesh. The vibration sends her over the edge, and she screams my name as she falls apart at my mercy.

I don't stop until she begs me to, and only then do I stand. Putting my fingers at her lips, I demand, "Suck."

Meri darts her tongue out of her mouth, swirling it around the tips before leaning forward and sucking like her life depends on it.

Fucking hell.

I thrust my cock against her stomach, and she nods as she releases my hand.

"I need you inside me, Poker," she purrs. "I need it so bad."

I lift her up and hold her with one arm, using my chest to help with leverage against the wall, while I guide my dick to her center.

"Oh," she moans when I push the tip in. "More."

Inch by granite-hard inch, I ease my way into her slick heat, and her head falls back.

"You take me so good," I groan as I move inside of her at a languid pace.

"Mmmm. More."

Unable to keep things slow, I increase my thrusts, jerking my hips forward to slam in balls deep. Each slap of skin is like a jolt to my nerve endings, and I'm buzzing with pleasure like I've never known.

Meri's nails dig into my back, and I almost hope she breaks skin so I can wear her mark.

"I'm so close," she whimpers.

"Touch yourself," I demand. "Take what you need to come again."

She slides one hand from my back, over my shoulder and down my chest until she reaches her clit. There's something about her small hand between us, both of us chasing our pleasure, that draws my balls tight.

"I'm…" Meri moans. "I'm…" She moans again. "I'm… Poker!"

She shatters around my cock, and that triggers my own release. Spots dance in front of my eyes, my soul rips clean open, and every ounce of energy flows from my body.

"Fuck," I say with a shudder as I slide out of her and set her on her feet.

When I'm sure we're both steady on our feet, I turn the shower off and lift her into my arms to carry her to the bed.

"Uh, what about drying off?" she asks, a teasing quality to her tone.

"Fuck it," I mutter. "I just wanna wrap myself around you."

"Okay."

We crawl under her sheet, and she wraps around me like a koala. "Thank you for that, Poker."

I stiffen. "You're thanking me for fucking you?"

"No. I'm thanking you for erasing him."

I relax. "Anytime, babe. As long as you have me, mine is the only touch you should ever experience."

CHAPTER 16
MERI

TOLD YOU I COULD TAKE CARE OF MYSELF.

One week later...

"I'M SO GLAD YOU CAME."

I smile at Ember over the bottle of beer I'm nursing. Contrary to popular belief, not all bartenders are lushes. I like to drink as much as the next chick, but I don't like to get sloppy. And since this is my first party at the Soulless Kings clubhouse, I'm being extra careful.

"Me too. I see you all at Ballinger's, but this is different."

She laughs. "You have no idea."

Poker and the other brothers have been sequestered in a room for the last hour, ever since Tracer ran into the common room yelling *I got him*. I assume he was referring to Diego, but I don't know if I'll ever get confirmation. I'm okay with that, though. Poker will tell me what I need to know.

"He'll be back soon," Addison says, following my gaze to the hallway where they disappeared.

"Am I that obvious?"

"Don't let them make you feel bad about wanting to be with your man," Wren, Journey's old lady says.

I know all about her multiple personalities, having witnessed her shift a few times at Ballinger's, but she seems to be doing well, and I'm happy for that. I can't imagine how hard Dissociative Identity Disorder is.

"It's just…"

"It's still new," Ember supplies when words fail me.

"Exactly. I've never been the type of girl who wants to spend all her time with a guy, but shit… Poker's different."

Ember sighs wistfully. "That's a biker for you. They're all different. But in a good way."

It's not five minutes later that the guys stroll into the large room, each making a beeline for either their woman, a Bangin' Betty, or the bar for a drink.

"Hey, babe," Poker greets as he slides an arm around the small of my back. "Having fun?"

"Yeah."

I search his eyes for the confirmation I want about Diego, and somehow, he knows exactly what I need and gives an almost imperceptible nod. Relief washes over me, and I take a long pull of my beer.

"Wanna shoot some pool?" he asks. "We could even put a little wager on it." Poker bobs his eyebrows suggestively.

"I'm game, but I've gotta warn you, I'm pretty fucking good."

"Is that so?" He grabs my hand and practically drags me toward the pool table across the room. "What are you willing to bet?"

Instinctively, I want to turn this into some version of strip poker, but we're not alone, so…

"For every ball I sink, you drink a shot of Jack."

"And for every ball I sink?"

"I'll down a Blowjob."

"Jesus," he rasps as he thrusts his hands through his hair. "You're on."

Two games later, I'm drunk as shit.

How the hell did that happen? I'm a pool goddess!

I sway as Poker guides me toward an empty couch, but halfway there, he stops in his tracks, and I slam against him.

"What're you doin'," I slur.

"Hey, baby," a woman's voice is the only response

I hear, and I immediately perk up. "How about you ditch drunk Barbie and take me to your room?"

Say what now?

"Kitty, you know that's not gonna happen," he snaps, keeping me tightly tucked to his side. "Move."

I manage to clear my vision by blinking several times, and that's when any trace of alcohol flees from my system.

This slut has her hands on my man!

I straighten to move in front of him, forcing her to break contact. "You heard him," I snarl. "Move."

"You think he's gonna stay with you? He's been fucking me for years," she taunts. "When he's sick of your rancid pussy, he'll come craw—"

Pain radiates through my hand and up my arm as my fist connects with her jaw, but I ignore it.

"The only rancid pussy here is yours!" I shout, punching her again. "Poker is taken, and it would be wise of you to remember that you fucking bitch." Hauling my arm back, I land another blow.

Kitty is now on the floor, trying to scramble away from me, but I bend down and grab her by the hair.

"Poker, help me!" she screams.

I glance over my shoulder to see him standing with his arms crossed over his chest and a grin on his face. "I'm good."

"Somebody, hel—"

Dropping her head, I stomp a foot into her chest, grinning sadistically when she writhes in pain. Then I yank her up by her hair again and drag her to the door. As soon as I have her outside, I let go, enjoying the thud of her thick skull on the pavement.

I turn around and storm back into the common room, and Poker is standing just inside the threshold. "Feel better?" he asks with a smirk.

"Told you I could take care of myself," I snap.

And then I promptly pass the fuck out.

CHAPTER 17
POKER

THERE IS NOTHING ON EARTH THAT COULD STOP ME FROM KEEPING HER.

TOLD YOU I COULD TAKE CARE OF MYSELF.

Meri's words echo in my mind as I lie here staring at the ceiling. The first hint of daylight streams through my window, casting a glow in the room. After she passed out last night, I carried her to my room and had Jackyl check her over to make sure she was okay. He assured me that she'd be fine once she got some rest, so I've been watching over her ever since.

When Kitty came up to me at the party, I was worried that Meri would mistake her advances for something I wanted, but my little hellcat surprised the fuck out of me.

And turned me on.

Meri stirs beside me, pulling me from the memory of the beat down she gave. She looks so good in my bed, sprawled out under my sheets, and it takes an unnatural amount of willpower not to ease my way inside of her body and wake her up with my dick.

"I'm never drinking again," she says, her tone groggy, as she moves her arm to cover her still closed eyes.

I chuckle. "That's what they all say."

Slowly, she lowers her arm and cracks open one eye. "Am... Where am I?"

"You don't remember?"

Oh, this is too good.

Meri shakes her head and winces. "Fuck, that hurts."

"I hate to be the bearer of bad news, but you died and went to Heaven."

Now both eyes are open, and she's squinting at me. "Makes sense."

Huffing out a laugh, I slip an arm beneath her and pull her against my side. "How does that make sense?"

"Because that's the only scenario I can think of where I'd feel this shitty while I'm with you."

"Am I death or Heaven?"

She playfully smacks my chest. "Heaven, of course."

"And how does beating Kitty and dragging her out of the clubhouse by her hair factor in?" I ask, humor lacing my words.

"Oh, God, that really happened?"

"Yep."

"Is Crow gonna kill me? He's probably gonna kill me. I don't blame him, I guess, because I caused a scene, and now he's gotta—"

I press a finger to her lips to stop her rambling. "Crow isn't gonna kill you," I assure her. "You didn't do anything wrong."

"But I interfered in club business."

I pull her to straddle me and cup her cheeks as I shake my head. "No, babe. That wasn't club business. That was personal, and you handled it like a pro."

"So, he's not mad?"

"Hell, no. If anything, he's as proud of you as I am."

She exhales a relieved breath. "That bitch just made me so fucking mad. I mean, who the hell hits on a guy who's clearly with another woman?"

"Trust me when I say, you have nothing to worry about when it comes to Kitty."

Meri locks eyes with me. "I know. I trust you."

That simple statement shoves me headfirst over the cliff of emotion I've been teetering on. If I wasn't in love with this woman before, I am now.

I clear my throat. "Besides, you'll never have to worry about Kitty again."

She gasps. "I didn't kill her, did I?"

I smile. "No."

She narrows her eyes. "You didn't kill her, did you?"

My smile turns into a full-blown grin. "No. No one killed anyone. But Kitty *has* been kicked out of the club and ordered to never show her face again."

"Oh." My girl seems almost disappointed by that news.

"She broke a major rule by disrespecting you, and she knew it. Don't feel bad for her."

"I don't, not really."

"Then what's wrong?"

"Nothing. I..." She swallows. "I just didn't expect to be treated like I'm one of you guys."

"Aw, babe, the second I set my sights on you, you became one of us."

She shifts to lie down on my chest, her cheek pressed against my heart. "I like that," she whispers, her breath kissing my skin.

It isn't more than a few minutes before her breathing evens out, and I know she's asleep again.

As I lie here and hold her, I think about how easily she's become the most important person in my world. I don't know what the fuck I ever did to deserve her, but I know that there is nothing on Earth that could stop me from keeping her.

CHAPTER 18
MERI

Yay me.

"Lock up behind me."

I roll my eyes at Poker. I spent the day with him at the clubhouse but insisted that I come home tonight since I didn't have any of my stuff, and he had club business to deal with. Maybe I need to talk to him about keeping a few changes of clothes and some toiletries at the clubhouse in case I stay again, but I decide to wait.

It's too soon... right?

"I will. Text me when you get home?"

He grins. "Worried about me?"

"Always," I admit.

"I could get used to that," he says.

"You probably should."

He chuckles. "I'll let you know when I'm home safe. Promise."

"Thanks."

"Just remember it might be a while," he reminds me. "I don't know how long business is gonna take."

"I know."

Poker kisses me deeply before turning and walking out my front door. I lock the door and make my way to my bedroom to change into a pair of sweats and a t-shirt. It feels good to be out of the clothes I had on last night, but it'd be better if I was still wearing the faded t-shirt Poker lent me.

Part of me wants to curl up in bed and sleep, but it's only seven, and I'm not quite old enough to be okay with going to bed before the sun. Instead, I take my cell and head to the living room and crawl beneath a blanket to watch a movie.

"Sweet Home Alabama" is one of my all-time favorite flicks, and I say the words along with the characters.

"'What, did they run outta soap down at the Piggly Wiggly since I left?'" Reese Witherspoon and I say simultaneously, and I laugh out loud.

"Wrong! The only reason I ain't signin' is cause you've turned into some hoity-toity Yankee bitch, and I'd like nothing better right now than to piss you off," Josh Lucas' character sneers a few frames later.

"You tell her," I mutter.

It's not until Josh and Reese's characters are standing on the beach in a storm at the end of the movie that my eyes begin to slowly close.

I don't know how long I sleep, but I'm startled awake by a pounding sound. It takes a moment to realize that someone is knocking at my door. No light streams through my windows, so I know it's late.

The knocking continues as I get to my feet. "I'm coming," I call, thinking maybe it's Poker.

He stops knocking at the sound of my voice. I unlock the door, a smile on my face, but it disappears the second I open the barrier because there's no one on my porch. I go to step outside, and my foot connects with something, pulling my attention downward.

On my welcome mat is a medium-size box with 'Meri' written on the top in black marker. Frowning, I pick it up and carry it inside. Returning to the couch, I set the box on the coffee table and peel the tape off to open it.

When I see what's inside, my stomach plummets. There's a green dress that's identical to the one I wore to my last poker game, but it's got slash marks cutting up the material. Under that, is a picture of Poker with a red 'X' over it. I set those two things aside and pull out the folded piece of paper at the bottom. I open it, and my heart joins my stomach.

Meri-
You didn't listen.
-D

Tossing the note onto the couch beside me as if it burned my fingers, I settle against the cushions. This has to be from Diego, but how did he get my home address? How did he know my real name? And what does he mean, I didn't listen? I gave Poker the message. I did what he demanded of me.

I grab my cell to call Poker but stop myself before hitting send. He said he had club business to deal with and promised to text when he got home. Since I don't have any texts from him yet, I know he's still busy. I decide to text him instead of calling, so I don't interrupt whatever it is he's doing.

> Meri: I need you to come back to the house when you can. Got another note. This time it came with a package. Yay me 🙁

CHAPTER 19
POKER

I won't let anyone hurt her, not as long as I have breath left in my body.

"You'll regret this."

Next to me, Ghost barks out a laugh while I simply stare at Diego. Tracer was able to determine that the brother he mentioned to Meri is Esteban. When I learned that, I'd been livid, but after some more digging and a meeting with Esteban, I was satisfied that Diego and Esteban aren't close, and Diego only wanted him alive so he could eliminate him and take over his arm of the cartel.

With Esteban's blessing and assistance, we located Diego, and he's now swinging naked from chains in the Nightmare Room.

"Ya think?" I finally counter. "Because I'm not sure I'm capable of the emotion."

Regret isn't something I allow myself to feel very often. In fact, I never feel it after taking out a threat.

"My brother will come for you," Diego sneers, blood dribbling down his torso from the shallow cuts I've made.

I look to Ghost. "Hear that, brother? He thinks Esteban gives a shit about him."

Ghost grins as he slides his gaze to our prisoner. "How do you think we found you, hmm?"

Diego visibly flinches but recovers quickly. "He wouldn't dare."

"Oh, he dared," I tell him. "It seems he's been keeping tabs on you for years. He knew you'd try something to get him out of your way, and he was right. But what you don't get is that he has some honor. He might not like the Soulless Kings, but unlike you, he wouldn't use a woman to get to us."

In reality, I have no clue how Esteban feels about the club. We have a precarious relationship with him, but honor is honor. I'll figure out everything beyond that after his attendance at the upcoming poker game. Right now, my sole focus is destroying Diego for daring to scare Meri. Besides, what's that saying?

The enemy of my enemy is my friend.

Right now, Diego is the enemy, and Esteban is the friend. We'll see how long that friendship lasts.

Diego opens his mouth to argue but doesn't get a word out because I haul my arm back and deliver a right hook to his jaw.

"The time for talking is over," I snarl. "Ghost, grab me the spiked bat."

The Sergeant at Arms snags the bat from its perch on the wall and hands it to me. The wooden weapon is covered with nails and wrapped in barbed wire. It's not a weapon I use often, but feeling its weight in my hands, I make a mental note to use it more.

"What the fuck is that?" Diego snaps, fear infusing his words.

I smile sadistically. "Well, it's two things really. It's one of my own creations and is designed to inflict the maximum amount of pain without always being fatal."

"And the second?" he asks warily.

"It's your murder weapon."

I swing the bat at his torso, making sure to drag the spikes along his skin and shredding him open. Over and over, I do this. I don't stop until my arms are heavy, and my chest is heaving.

Diego has passed out, and that's fine with me. I didn't need any information from him, just needed him to suffer. Before I toss the bat to the floor, I swing it at his head until his skull is caved in, and I'm sure he's dead.

"Fuck, that was fun," I say gleefully when I'm done.

"I'll take your word for it," Ghost mutters.

I turn to face him. "What's your problem?"

"You didn't even let me get in one hit," he whines.

"Jesus, grow a pair," I taunt. "You can have the next son of a bitch."

He throws up his arms and stalks out of the room, clearly annoyed. He'll get over it, though. This was my kill.

As I make my way upstairs, my phone vibrates in my pocket, and I pull it out. When I see the text from Meri, my adrenaline spikes.

I race out of the clubhouse and climb on my Harley. After shooting her a quick text to let her know I'm on my way, I peel away from the building.

It takes me fifteen minutes to get to her house, but it might as well be an eternity. Meri answers the door quickly, like she was standing right there just waiting for me. I immediately gather her in my arms and guide her to the couch.

"You're okay," I murmur against her hair, although I think it's more for my benefit than hers.

She nods against me. "Show me the package," I demand after I'm satisfied that she's alright.

Meri pulls away from me and points to the box on the coffee table. I was so tuned in to her that I didn't even notice it.

"It has to be from Diego. That's the only thing that makes sense. He brought this shit to my house and disappeared like a coward before I could confront him."

I take in the contents of the box, as well as the short note, and my vision blurs with fury. "It wasn't Diego," I seethe.

"How do you know?" she counters. "I mean, I know I didn't see who delivered it, but it's signed 'D'. And the note suggests it's him."

"I guess he could've had someone else bring it," I allow. "But he's not who was here."

"But how do y—"

"Diego's dead," I blurt. At her shocked expression, I thrust a hand through my hair and heave a sigh. "I've been with him for the last few hours, so I know he couldn't have brought it here himself. And if he is behind the contents, he's dead and no longer a problem."

She eyes me curiously. "Okay. I'm guessing this isn't something I should ask questions about."

I smirk. "Probably not."

"Fine." Her tone is clipped, but there's no heat behind the word. She might not like it, but she understands. Meri rubs her temples. "None of this makes sense, Poker. This makes three notes. The flowers, the one on my door, and this. All of them are signed by different people. What the fuck is going on?"

"I don't know, but we're gonna figure it out, okay?" She nods. "Go grab whatever you need for the night. You're coming back to the clubhouse with me. We'll sort this out and get a game plan."

I expect her to put up a fight, but she doesn't. Thirty minutes later, we're strolling through the clubhouse toward the meeting room. I texted Crow before we left her house to call church so everyone would be ready when we arrived. I also got his permission to bring Meri into the meeting because only she can answer some of our questions.

"Hey, Meri," Crow greets when we walk into the room. "You okay?"

"I'm fine. Just pissed."

"Pissed is good," Journey tells her.

"Pissed will keep you alive," Screamer adds.

"Jesus, you think someone wants to kill me?" she asks.

"We don't know," Ghost states. "But that's what we're gonna figure out."

Only, we don't figure shit out. By the time church is over, the only thing we're sure of is I'm staying with Meri at her place until further notice. She quickly agreed, which surprised me, but I don't question her reasoning. We'll put in a security system, and one of the brothers will be outside on guard duty any time she's home, whether I'm there or not.

We discuss the possibility that this has something to do with the club, especially since my picture was included in the package from tonight, but it doesn't seem likely. Everything so far has been geared toward Meri, and it started before she and I were together.

As of now, we're operating under two possibilities: This is one person who is trying to throw us off by using different initials, or this is multiple people working together to cause the most amount of fear and destruction.

Either way, Meri will walk away from this whole. I won't let anyone hurt her, not as long as I have breath left in my body.

CHAPTER 20
MERI

I FOCUS ON ALL THE WAYS THIS MAN INVADES MY SENSES AND IGNORE THE FACT THAT THERE'S SOMEONE OUT THERE WHO'S HELLBENT ON TERRORIZING ME.

Two weeks later...

"Everything okay with you?"

I smile reassuringly at Lance. He seems to have finally gotten the hint that I'm not interested, and now that there isn't tension between us, he's actually a pretty nice guy.

"All good," I say.

And it is... sort of.

Poker has been living with me since the night I received the package. It took a few days for us to get into a routine, but now it feels like we've been together forever. I like having him in my space, like having his clothes mixed with mine in the laundry and his toothbrush next to mine in the ceramic holder on my bathroom counter. I like it so much that I'm not sure what I'll do when he goes back to the clubhouse.

Probably curl up in a ball and cry.

"You sure?" Lance asks. "Because if you need to talk, I'm here."

"I'm sure, but thank you," I say.

He disappears into the kitchen, leaving me to my thoughts.

It's not Poker living with me that's the problem. It's everything else. Esteban attended the poker game two nights ago, as did Mr. Neero. Poker and I questioned Neero about the note that was taped to my door, the one signed 'N', and we're both satisfied that he had nothing to do with it. The man's a jackass, but that and terrible business practices are all he's guilty of.

So, who's doing this?

That's what has me so on edge. I was hoping that meeting Esteban would provide more clues, especially since Poker seemed so unsure of him, but he's not the threat. At least, we don't think so. And neither does the club.

After the game, we went straight to the clubhouse. I'd allowed Poker to set up cameras and recording devices at the game, and his brothers were able to watch everything live. Esteban was a perfect gentleman, and Poker said that his gut told him Esteban isn't involved. That seemed to be enough for the brothers, and it's enough for me.

With each new note, we've all been thinking that there are multiple senders. But now, I'm sure there aren't. But who would be doing this and purposely try to mislead us?

That's the million-dollar question.

"Hey, babe."

Poker's greeting yanks me from my thoughts, and I smile at him. "Hi."

"Whatcha thinking about?"

"Do you really need to ask me that?" I counter.

His grin falls. "No, I guess not."

"Sorry. I'm just… Dammit, why can't we figure this out?"

He reaches across the bar and grabs my hand to bring it to his lips. After kissing my knuckles, he rests our joined hands on the bar top. "Your shift's over in ten. Think you can cut out early?"

"Yeah. We're not busy. Lance can cover."

I go to the break room to grab my purse. When I return to the bar area, Lance is just coming out of the kitchen.

"Hey, you mind if I cut out?" I ask him.

"No, go ahead."

"Thanks. I'll let Grady know I left early." My boss won't give a damn about ten minutes, but I'll text him all the same.

"Sounds good."

Poker and I walk out of Ballinger's, stopping at my car. His eyes narrow dangerously, and I follow his line of sight to a piece of paper tucked under my windshield wiper.

"You've gotta be kidding me," I groan.

He snatches the paper and unfolds it so we can both read whatever is on it.

> *M-*
> *You're making things worse for yourself. The company you keep, the people you let into your life... You should be more careful. Ditch the biker and all those other rich bastards. I promise, I'll make it worth it. You'll be mine, and I'll be yours. Do it quick before it's too late.*
> *-E*

Poker darts his eyes up and down the street as if looking for any sign of the letter-writer. His muscles are bunched under his short-sleeved t-shirt and cut, and he's coiled tighter than a rattler ready to strike.

"Do you think it was Esteban?" I ask, already knowing the answer.

"No." He wraps his arm around my shoulder as he tucks the note away in his back pocket. "I'll find out for sure, but I really don't think so. Whoever it is, it's the same person writing all of them. They want us running in a million different directions."

"But who?"

He looks me in the eye and scowls. "I don't know."

The weight in those words kills me. Not because he hasn't figured it out, but because he's trying so hard *to* figure it out... for me.

"C'mon," he says, pulling me away from my car. "I'll have one of the prospects pick up your vehicle and bring it home. I'm not letting you out of my sight right now."

"Okay."

After helping me onto his Harley, he climbs on in front of me. The ride to my house goes by in a blur. I force myself to focus on the touch of his hand on my thigh, the warmth seeping from his body to mine, the rumble of the bike beneath me. I focus on all the ways this man invades my senses and ignore the fact that there's someone out there who's hellbent on terrorizing me.

CHAPTER 21
POKER

It's fucking important.

"It wasn't me. I may be an evil man, but even I draw the line at scaring or hurting women and children."

Esteban's voice is firm, and I believe him. I never really thought it was, but I had to be sure.

"I figured," I admit.

When we got back to Meri's house, she was wound so tight, it took a few hours for her to relax enough and fall asleep. She kept telling me she was okay, only angry, but I could see her fear, see the panic in her eyes at every little noise.

As soon as she was out, I came to the living room to make my call.

"Is there anything I can do to be of assistance?" Esteban asks.

We're not exactly allies, but we're not enemies either. After this week's poker game, I'm sure of that. As sure as a man can be anyway.

"I'll let you know."

"Please do."

I'm about to end the call, but a thought occurs to me. "Hey, man, real quick…"

"Yes?"

"Could this be in any way related to the street dealers that were eliminated for poaching our brand?"

I know the answer, but I'm running out of ideas.

"No. Based on what you've told me, this started before that."

"Right. Had to ask."

"I know." Esteban sighs, making him seem more relatable somehow. "Poker, if this were my woman, I'd be looking at the men in her life."

"We are. But we're also digging into connections to the club. We can't ignore that it's her association with me that's put her in this position."

"I'll do some checking with my contacts. Might be easier for me to flush out your enemies."

"Thanks, I appreciate that."

"In the meantime, you focus on Meri and her

acquaintances. Experience tells me it's a man, but I suppose it could be a woman."

That thought hadn't occurred to me. "Thanks again. Call me if you find anything."

"I will."

After disconnecting that call, I make another.

"It's fucking late," Crow snarls after three rings.

"And it's fucking important," I snap.

The rustle of sheets comes through the line, and a few seconds later, it's followed by the sound of a door shutting, which tells me he got out of bed and left the room, so he doesn't wake Addison.

"I'm listening," he finally says.

I fill him in on the note that was left on Meri's windshield and my phone call with Esteban. He's quiet as I speak, but I know him. His mind is anything but quiet.

"You called Esteban before you called me?" he asks when I'm done speaking.

Shit.

"I did," I confirm.

Crow sighs. "I get it. Meri's your girl, and you're pissed. But next time, I'm your first call, got it?"

"Understood."

"Besides, I coulda told you it wasn't him."

"I didn't really think it was."

"So, what's the plan?"

"You don't wanna take it to the club?"

"Oh, we'll be taking it to the club," Crow says. "But right now, I'm asking you."

"Esteban suggested that we look into any man in her life. I think he's right. We can rule out me and anyone in the club, but what about people from Ballinger's or her games?"

"I agree. I'll talk to Grady and see if he's okay with us being more present at the bar and if there's anyone he can think of as a threat to Meri. As for the games, that's your domain. You can have some of the guys handle security for them until this is over, but how do you think she'll feel about that?"

"I think she'll be fine. I'm more worried about her security team in case it's one of them."

"I'll have Tracer dig a little deeper into them. He hasn't found anything yet, but who knows?"

"Okay. I'll discuss all this with Meri when she wakes up. It took her forever to fall asleep, so I want to let her be."

"We'll figure this out, brother," Crow assures me. "Nothing will happen to her."

"I know."

"Look, try to get some sleep. There's nothing you can do right now, and you'll be no good to her exhausted."

"Yeah."

After hanging up, I make my way back to the bedroom and slide under the sheet, wrapping my arm around Meri. I'm fully expecting to remain awake, but it isn't long before my eyelids grow heavy, and sleep pulls me under.

CHAPTER 22
MERI

I'M NOT JEALOUS, JUST POSSESSIVE.

"He'll get over it."

I focus on the feel of Poker's hand settled on my hip. It's been another two weeks since the last note, and we're no closer to figuring out the mystery. Tonight, Conrad and a few of the club brothers are providing security, but apparently, not everyone on my security team is happy with this arrangement.

"Was Solomon okay with it?" I ask, wanting to forget about Malcolm's ire.

"Both he and Grant were fine," Conrad assures us. "As for Malcolm, he's beating himself up for letting that guy, Diego, slip past him to your office, and he feels like he's being punished."

"He's not being punished. As for letting Diego

slip by, that was all of you," Poker states, asserting his position as the man by my side and in charge of my safety. "Don't think for a second that either of us thinks otherwise."

"Poker, please," I whisper.

He squeezes my side reassuringly. "I know, I know. You can handle this."

My lips curve into a smile. While I appreciate his protection, it's not his place to condemn my people.

"Where do you want us, Meri?" Screamer asks when he joins our group of three.

"Mistress Green," Conrad corrects. "Here, she's Mistress Green."

"My bad," Screamer says. "Where do you want us, Mistress Green?"

I shake my head. "If you, Ghost, Jackyl, and Python could spread out at the perimeter of the room, that'd be great. Conrad will cover the door, as the players are familiar with him. Poker, you'll be at the table as a player, and Journey will be at the bar. Oh, and Tracer and Stunner will be flanking me."

The men nod, and Conrad and Screamer walk away with their marching orders.

"You okay?" Poker asks me when we're alone.

"Yeah."

And I am for the most part. I don't think anything

will happen during one of my games, but all this planning and security is weighing on me.

Poker lets his gaze travel from my face, down the length of my body, and back up again. "Have I told you yet how stunning you look in this dress?"

I'm wearing my emerald green one with the high slit and deep plunging front. It makes me feel sexy, and feeling sexy is a confidence booster.

"Oh, only about five times since I put it on."

"As soon as we get back to your place, it's coming off, understood?"

My clit throbs. "Yes, sir."

"Fuck," he rasps. "C'mon."

He practically drags me to my office. Kicking the door shut, he spins us around and slams me against it before shoving his hand past the slit in my dress.

"You're so wet," he growls, as he slides my thong aside to plunge a finger into my heat.

"Fuck me, Poker," I beg. "Please fuck me."

He quickly undoes his pants and pushes them and his boxer briefs over his hips, and they bunch at his knees. In the next second, he's thrusting into me. I stretch around him, his cock snug in my pussy.

"So fucking good," he says with his face pressed against my throat.

There is nothing slow or loving about this, but the fast, hard, desperate pace of it is exactly what I need.

Poker presses a thumb to my clit, rubbing fast circles with his thumb, and I detonate.

My pussy spasms, and his cock pulses with our shared release. As soon as we're both done, he kisses me. Now this, this is slow and loving.

"We should probably get out there," I say when I ease away from him.

"We should."

"I want to do that again."

"Oh, don't you worry, babe," he teases. "We'll be doing that again as soon as we're home."

"Promise?"

"Promise."

Entering the main room, I see that all the invitees have arrived and are sitting at the table waiting for me. None of them brought a plus one, which makes security easier because that means no unknowns.

"'Bout time," Martin mutters when I reach my place. His gaze shifts to Poker when he takes his chair. "Should he really be playing since it's clear the two of you are together?"

"If you have a problem with it, feel free to leave," I say.

"I can keep my personal life out of the game," Poker adds, addressing Martin. "Can you?"

"What's that supposed to mean?" the man demands, bristling.

Poker shrugs. "It means exactly what you think it means. Is there a reason you feel threatened that I'm still here while bangin' the host?"

"Poker," I admonish in a harsh whisper.

"No, I don't feel threatened," Martin says. "It's just a conflict of interest. But if everyone else is okay with it, then so am I."

"Anyone else have a problem with it?" Poker asks, shifting his gaze from one player to the next.

"The only problem I have," Ms. Rogers begins. "Is that you're with her and not me."

"Careful, Ms. Rogers," Poker says. "The last woman who hit on me ended up on the receiving end of Mistress Green's wrath."

The woman has the audacity to laugh. "Oh, I think I can take her."

She turns in her chair and flattens her palms on Poker's chest, and I see red.

"Get out," I bark.

Poker grins, and Ms. Rogers glances at me. "Excuse me?"

"You heard me," I snap. "Get the fuck out."

When she makes no move to obey, Stunner and Tracer take menacing steps forward.

"You heard her," Stunner says.

"But I paid to be here," she argues.

"I don't give a fuck if you gave up your first born

to be here," I snarl. "You touched my man, and I won't stand by and let it pass. Get the fuck out, and never come back."

It's then that Journey comes from his position at the side of the room and practically yanks her to her feet. "Shoulda done this the easy way, lady," he mutters.

I return my attention to the others. "Now, is everyone ready to get started?"

Fortunately, that incident is the only one of the night. Poker throws a few hands to appease Martin, but it's Ms. Graven, who walks away the clear winner for the evening.

"You really know how to turn me on," Poker tells me as we walk to his matte black Camaro after everyone else leaves."

"You're talking about me kicking out Ms. Rogers, aren't you?"

He grins. "What can I say? Jealousy looks good on you."

I throw my head back and laugh. "I'm not jealous, just possessive."

"Hmm, me too."

CHAPTER 23
POKER

I NEED TO GET TO MERI.

MERI'S ARMS TIGHTEN AROUND MY WAIST AS WE LEAN into the curve. It's her day off, and we decided to go for a ride. About two hours away from Marble Falls, we stopped in a little town to eat lunch at a small diner, then we walked down their Main Street, going from one shop to the next.

I've never been the shopping type, or even the exploring a new town type, but with Meri, everything is fun.

We're fifteen miles from Marble Falls, and traffic is light, so when a dark sedan seems to come up on us out of nowhere, the hair on the back of my neck stands on end.

I wrap my hand around Meri's thigh, reassuring

myself that she's okay, and then I increase my speed. The sedan speeds up to stay on my tail, and genuine fear slithers through me. Going out on my Harley is not something I've ever been afraid of, but with Meri on the back of my bike, the idea of it is inconceivable.

After two vehicles pass us going the other direction, the sedan swerves into the oncoming lane, and before I can figure out what they're doing, the driver yanks the wheel and slams into our side.

I try to maintain control, but it's impossible. My bike has a mind of its own. I engage the brakes, doing as much damage control as I can, but it's too late. The bike tips and skids to a halt on the asphalt, throwing both of us off to barrel into the ditch.

Meri's scream pierces the air, and pain shoots through my body. Fortunately, we both were wearing helmets since it was a longer ride, but there's no telling what kind of injuries we've sustained.

"Meri," I call out, unable to see her. Not only is my vision blurry, but unconsciousness threatens to take over. Somehow, my bike managed to land on top of me, pinning me to the ground.

"P-Poker?" she says, her voice shaky. "Are you okay?"

"I think so, but I'm stuck. You?"

"Pretty banged up, but I-I don't think any-anything is broken. My head is s-spinning though."

"Ok. Just stay calm," I order. "I'm going to try to get to my cell and see if I can get us some help."

I don't get a response.

"Meri?" Nothing. "Meri!"

When she remains quiet, terror claws at my insides, making it even harder to breathe. A shadow falls over me, and for a split-second, I feel relief because someone will help us. But it's short-lived whenever the person walks away.

I try to twist and turn to get my cell, but nothing works. Then an idea hits me.

"Siri!" I shout, hoping like fucking hell that damn faceless AI bitch can hear me. "Call Crow!"

"Calling Crow," the robotic voice replies.

I clearly can't hear if he answers, so all I can do is shout 'help' over and over, hoping he hears me. I shout it until my throat dries to the point that I can't speak, and then the dark sucks me under.

"I'M SORRY, BROTHER."

Crow.

Those are the first words I hear when I open my eyes, and my heart cracks wide open.

She's dead.

"No," I whisper, shaking my head and ignoring the way the movement makes it feel like bowling balls are rattling around in my skull. "No, no, no."

"I'm sure if you talk to her, make her see reason, you can work it out," Crow says.

Grief overwhelms me, and I thrash on the bed in an effort to escape it, but after several seconds, his words penetrate the fog.

I'm sure if you talk to her…

I whip my gaze to Pres. "What did you say?" I demand.

He stares at me with confusion. "I'm sure that if you talk to Meri, she'll come around, and the two of you will work it out."

"She's not dead?"

"What?" He balks. "No, she's very much alive. She's just not… here."

I sag against the pillow with relief. "Fucking hell, Crow," I snarl. "You scared the shit out of me."

"Sorry, I thought you knew."

"I didn't. She stopped responding to me before I called you."

"Shit. Sorry, man."

"Wait," I say. "She's not here?"

He looks away from me. "No. She left two days ago."

"Two days!" I roar. *Fuck that hurts.* "How long has it been since the wreck?"

"Um... Three days."

I throw the sheet off and swing my legs over the edge of the bed. Dizziness plagues me, and Crow pushes me back down.

"You're not going anywhere until Jackyl clears you," he orders.

"Fuck that," I bark as I try to struggle against him. Unfortunately, I'm not at my strongest yet and get nowhere. Giving up, I flop down. "Why'd she leave?" I finally ask.

"First things first," he begins. "I know when you come to your senses, this would've been a better question. Meri suffered from a concussion, and Jackyl monitored her overnight. She's got a lot of scrapes and bruises, but physically, she's fine."

Dammit, I let my grief and then anger completely obliterate rational thought. Of course, I should've asked that first.

"That's good."

"It's pretty much the same for you, but you were in and out of consciousness until now. We were worried about you, but Jackyl said you just needed to give your brain a rest."

"Okay, fine. My brain rested," I huff out. "Now, why'd she leave?"

Crow reaches into his pocket and pulls out a piece of paper. Instantly, I'm on the ragged edge of fury.

"This was sitting on your bike when we got to you."

He hands it to me, and I mentally brace myself for what I'm going to read.

> Poker-
> Why isn't anyone taking me seriously? I've sent warnings and threats, but you're both still too stupid to listen. I hope this is the wake up call you need and that your injuries aren't too bad.
> -R

"This one's addressed to me," I say unnecessarily.

"And that's what freaked Meri out. "Seems she's okay when she's the target, but put you in the line of fire, and she draws the line."

"Fuck!" I yell. "Who is doing this?"

"I don't know, man, but they're escalating. Running you both off the road? That's a declaration of war."

"How the hell can we fight a war when we don't even know who we're fighting against?" I ask, dejected.

He's silent, knowing my question is rhetorical.

"I need to talk to Meri," I spit out and try to sit up again.

Again, Crow pushes me to my back. "You can go to her when Jackyl clears you medically. That's not up for debate."

"I can't leave her alone, unprotected."

"Do you really think I'd do that? Shit, I've got two men at the front of her house and two in the back. She's safe."

"What about when she goes to Ballinger's?"

"She's taking some time off," he tells me. "That was the only way I'd let her walk out of the clubhouse."

"That's something, I guess," I mutter.

"Look, I've got shit to do, but I'll be back later to check on you." He starts for the door. "And Poker?"

"Yeah, Pres?"

"I've got Jackyl and Jimmy posted at your door, so don't even think about trying to take off."

With that, he's gone.

Shit, shit, shit. I need to get out of here. I need to get to Meri.

Now that I'm awake, surely Jackyl will clear me.
Right?
Wrong.

It's another two days before I'm able to leave the

clubhouse.

CHAPTER 24
MERI

He's the best damn Tootsie Pop ever made.

It's been four days since I walked out of the Soulless Kings clubhouse. Four days that I've been alone, in pain both physically and emotionally, marinating in my own misery.

Poker's called and texted numerous times, and I've ignored him each time. It's not that I don't want to talk to him, I do. I just don't want him to talk me out of my decision. The second I hear his voice or see him, I'll cave, and I can't do that.

Right now, Poker's the one who needs protection… from me.

A knock on my door pulls me from my thoughts, and I roll my eyes. Ghost and

Screamer are on guard duty this morning at the

front of my house, and I already told them they could come in anytime to get something to eat or drink or to use the restroom.

"It's open," I call from my spot on the couch.

I don't bother hiding the used Kleenex or feel ashamed about the empty pizza box and take-out containers scattered around. I just don't have it in me to care.

Miserable. I'm fucking miserable.

"This certainly isn't what I expected."

I sit up so fast, my head spins. Poker is standing at the end of my couch, arms crossed over his muscled chest.

"W-what are you doing here?" I find the presence of mind to ask.

"I could ask you the same thing," he snaps. "You left me, Meri. Explain."

"Didn't Crow already tell you?"

"I wanna hear it out of you."

I sigh. I should've known he'd do this. "Your life is in danger because of me, Poker. We could've died in that wreck," I practically screech. "What about that do you not get?"

"I don't get why you fucking left me!" he shouts.

Anger bubbles beneath my skin, and I shoot to my feet. "I left to keep you safe! This is happening because of me. You almost died because of me." Tears fill my eyes as I continue. "I wouldn't have been able to live with myself if that happened. You say you'll protect me, but dammit, I can protect you too."

Poker closes the distance between us and yanks me against his chest, wrapping his arms around me. "Shh, babe. It's okay. Everything is going to be okay."

Sobs burst from me, uncontrollable, filled with anguish and fear.

I don't know how long he holds onto me, but at some point, he lifts me off my feet and carries me to my bedroom. After gently setting me on the mattress, he climbs in with me, curling me into his side.

"Meri, you can't leave me like that," he says, his voice cracking with emotion. "Babe, I thought you were dead. When I woke up, and you weren't there, I thought you'd died."

I lift myself up onto my elbow and wipe the wetness from my cheeks. "I'm s-sorry. That wasn't my intention."

"I know, but fuck. I was... fuck."

"Poker, I just..." I shake my head to clear the cobwebs. "I *will* die if anything happens to you because of me. I... I love you."

His eyes widen, and a grin spreads across his features. "I love you, too, Meri. So goddamn much."

"Then you have to understand," I plead. "When I saw the note was addressed to you, all I could see were bad outcomes. Nothing but terrible outcomes that I don't know how to prevent. And all of it because of me."

"None of this is your fault," he snaps. "The blame belongs on whoever is sending the notes. Them and no one else."

"That doesn't change the fact that you got hurt."

"You're right, it doesn't. And it doesn't change the fact that you got hurt, too. But the only way either of us is going to get through it is if we stick together. What we have is good, Meri. It's so damn good. If we let them break that, they win."

"I'm so sorry, Poker. Can you forgive me?"

"As long as you promise to never leave me again," he says. "I can forgive you anything but that."

"I promise. If I get scared or start having doubts, I'll talk to you about it."

"Good." He grins. "Now, having you this close is doing things to me, babe. Wicked things."

He flips to his side so he's facing me and begins to slowly strip my clothes from my body. When I'm down to my sensible cotton panties—I wasn't planning on company… sue me—I stop him by scooting off the other side of the bed.

"What are you doing?"

"I think I need to express my apologies a little

better," I purr as I walk around to his side of the bed, pushing my panties over my hips as I go.

"How are you planning on doing that?"

After kicking my legs free of the panties, I lean over and start to undress him. One article of clothing at a time, I bare his gorgeous body to me. His muscles flex and his skin ripples as he watches me.

"Meri," he groans when I press my lips to his exposed stomach. "What are you doing to me?"

Flicking my eyes to his, I whisper huskily, "Licking you like a lollipop."

I sink my mouth around his hard cock, and his salty flavor bursts on my tongue. Moving to kneel between his legs, I lick and suck his length like he's the best damn Tootsie Pop ever made. Hell, he's better.

When he starts to thrust between my lips, fucking my throat with abandon, I cup his balls and roll them around in my hand.

"Jesus fucking Christ," he moans, his hands fisting in my hair. "I'm gonna come down that pretty throat of yours. You ready, babe?"

I slide off his cock, keeping only his tip between my lips, and nod. Just as his body jerks, I slam back down, and he explodes.

Poker stills after several seconds, and I swallow

every last drop of him before releasing his dick and moving back to curl into his side.

"I love being a lollipop," he says seriously.

I burst into laughter, and he quickly joins me.

"I love licking them," I tease.

We lie there for a while, neither of us speaking. Simply being with each other is enough. I don't know how much time passes, but at some point, both our phones ding with a notification. Mine is on my nightstand, and his is in his cut.

Both of us retrieve our devices, and a second later, I'm frozen, and Poker is muttering a string of curse words.

> Unknown: M&P- You will pay. -S

CHAPTER 25
POKER

When it's over, I'm still going to love you, and I'm still going to want you.

"Shut the hell up so we can get started!"

I shove my fingers between my lips and let loose a loud whistle after Crow's shouted order. All eyes turn to our president.

"That's better, now sit. We've got a lot to cover."

I pull Meri onto my lap, needing her close. Crow approved her being in church since she's as deep in this as the rest of us. I hate that we still need her to help figure this out, but we do.

"Poker, go ahead," Journey instructs.

"We got a sixth message last night," I start. "This time it was signed 'S'. We still think this is one person, but we don't know who."

"I've done deeper dives into your security team, Meri," Tracer says. "I'm not finding anything that stands out."

"So, we can rule them out," she says, relief in her tone.

"Not necessarily," Ghost states. "It just means they aren't likely suspects. But until we know for sure, we aren't ruling *anyone* out one hundred percent."

She nods in understanding.

"Tracer, can you put all the notes up on the screen so we can see them all side by side?" I ask.

He connects his laptop to the projector, and it's only moments before we can all see what he can see.

"We've all gone over these letters many times, but we're missing something," Screamer says, frustration in his tone.

"I've run them through different programs to see if there's a hidden code, but nothing pops," Tracer explains.

The room grows quiet as we stare at the notes, but then Meri's hand goes to her mouth, and she jumps to her feet and races to the screen.

"What're you seeing?" Crow asks.

"I don't…" She shakes her head. "Look," she orders, pointing to each note one at a time. "A-N-D-E-R-S."

"That mean something to you?" I ask.

"It's a name," she says. "Specifically, a last name."

"Spit it out, woman," Python snaps, and I whip my head in his direction.

"Speak to her like that again, and you'll have no hands left to tattoo with," I seethe.

Python lifts his hands. "Sorry."

"It's fine," Meri assures him. "He's just cranky." I growl, and the little minx grins. Then she sobers and takes a deep breath. "Anders is Malcolm's last name."

"Malcolm, from your security team?" I ask, and she nods. "It makes sense that it would be him. All of the notes were signed with an initial that could've matched a player. Wait... The 'A'? Who did you think that was?"

"Addison," Meri admits. "I got them right after she came with you, and since it just said 'thank you for an entertaining evening', she was my assumption."

"I can see that." Shifting my attention to Tracer, I ask, "Nothing popped with Malcolm?"

"Not a damn thing. He was raised by his father, got good grades in school, and was captain of the football team. He enlisted right out of high school and served four years in the Air Force. I'm assuming that's what made him a good hire for the security team. Dude doesn't have so much as a parking ticket."

"I find that hard to believe," I muse.

Tracer shrugs. "Malcolm could just be your run-of-the-mill creep."

"This actually makes me feel better," Meri says, returning to my lap.

"You feel better about this?" Crow asks.

"Yeah, I mean, think about it. If he's a run-of-the-mill creep, that means we can use run-of-the-mill ways to get him, right?"

"Whaddya have in mind?" Journey questions.

Meri scoffs like it should be obvious. "Get him at the next game. There's no way he knows we're onto him. All I have to do is tell him that we're returning to business as usual, and he'll be there."

"I'm not leaving you there without club protection," I bark.

"I figured you'd say that," she says sweetly. "You'll be there, of course, and we

can put two brothers in the game as well. He doesn't know who all of you are."

"Why can't we just use all club brothers play? That way we don't put anyone else in the crossfire," Jackyl suggests.

"Because he needs to see people he's familiar with," I explain before Meri can. "He's not stupid, which he's proved with all of this shit. If he even suspects that something is off, it could all go to hell in a handbasket."

"Okay, we'll have Poker, Stunner, and Ghost participate in the game," Crow says. "The rest of us will be on coms down the road in case things go sideways. All in favor, thump twice."

Every man in the room pounds the table twice. Belatedly, Meri does the same, eliciting a round of laughter.

"As far as being down the road, you don't have to do that," Meri explains. "There's another part of the warehouse that I did nothing with when I bought it, and at the back ar—"

"Wait, you own the warehouse?" I ask.

"Yep. I didn't want to risk the cops showing up and adding squatting to my list of crimes." She shrugs like it's nothing. "I'm a rich woman, Poker. Get over it."

"I'm not… I don't…"

"It's okay, I'll be your sugar mama," she teases.

Another round of laughter breaks out.

"Oh my God, that's the best thing I've heard in a long time," Screamer says between laughs.

"Shut the fuck up," I snap.

"Anyway," Meri says like she's speaking to children. "There are large sliding doors at the back of the building, so you can easily get your bikes inside to hide them. Malcolm sometimes walks the perimeter with Conrad, but none of the guys ever go into this other section. It's also accessible through a hidden door in the wall. I'm the only one who knows about it."

"A hidden door?"

Meri grins. "Yep. I did some research on it when I bought the place, and apparently the factory that used to operate there was in its prime during prohibition, so the workers installed the door so they could smuggle booze to the good people of Marble Falls."

"That's brilliant," Python says with admiration.

"And beneficial for us," Meri quips.

"Sounds like we've got a plan," Crow says. "Anything else we need to discuss?" When no one says anything, he continues. "Church dismissed."

When Meri and I are alone, I hold her close. "Feeling better?"

"I am. It's finally going to be over."

"Yes, it is."

Insecurity passes over her eyes. "What's wrong, babe?"

"What if this all ends and so do we? What if this is what brought us together? What i—"

I silence her with a quick press of my lips. When I

lean back, I level my gaze on hers. "I love you, Meri. This entire situation doesn't define us. It never has. It's a bump in the road. When it's over, I'm still going to love you, and I'm still going to want you. I guess the question is, are you still going to love me?"

"Always."

CHAPTER 26
MERI

Have you ever regretted taking the life of someone who's evil?

"He's not answering his phone, Mistress."

I sigh as if I have the weight of the world on my shoulders. This was all supposed to end tonight, but Malcolm hasn't bothered to show up.

What the hell? Does he know we know?

"Thank you, Conrad," I say. "We can't wait any longer, so I'll go ahead and get the game started."

We made the decision not to bring Conrad, Solomon, and Grant in on our plan because we didn't want to risk any of them collapsing under the pressure, so I know they didn't tip Malcolm off.

"Okay," Conrad says. "Maybe he's still upset about not being a part of the last few games."

"Maybe," I mutter.

When I reach the poker table inside, I do my best not to focus on Stunner and Ghost. I've never seen either of them in black tie apparel, and I can't deny that they're both gorgeous men, but I've only got eyes for Poker.

I deal the first round of cards. "Mr. Neero, it's your bet."

A few hands go by, and all seems to be running smoothly. Esteban, Mr. Neero, Ms. Graven, and Stefan are the players in attendance. As I'm dealing the fifth game, a gunshot rings out a second before an explosion takes out the warehouse entrance.

That's when everything turns to shit.

The four regular players dive under the table while Poker and his brothers jump to their feet and grab the weapons we attached to their chairs so Conrad wouldn't find them during his security search upon entry.

I grab my gun from the thigh holster I'm wearing, and point it in the direction of the door, just as the hidden door opens and Crow, Journey, Python, Jackyl, Screamer, and Tracer stride into the large space.

"What the fuck?" Crow shouts.

"I only want Mistress Green!" Malcolm yells as he seems to materialize from the smoke.

"Where's Conrad, Malcolm?" I demand.

"Dead."

Shit.

"You're not gonna get away with this," Poker snarls as he slowly eases toward me.

Malcolm laughs. "I already have. This place is rigged to blow if I don't get what I want."

"And you want me?" I ask.

"That's all I've ever wanted," he confirms. "It never should've gotten to this point. All you had to do was see me, like me, *need* me."

"Why didn't you just flirt with me like a normal person?" I snap. "Or, I don't fucking know, ask me out on a date?"

"Because you were always mooning over *him*," he sneers, nodding at Poker. "Filthy criminal biker can't give you the life I can."

"Uh, buddy," Poker comments dryly. "Hate to break it to you, but you're a criminal too. And so is she."

Malcolm frantically shakes his head. "No, no, no! I did all of this for love! It can't be criminal if it's for love!" He takes a few deep breaths, seemingly trying to gain some composure. Eventually, he focuses on me. "Come with me," he pleads. "Come with me, and we can put this behind us."

"No, Malcolm. I don't love you. Shit, right now I

don't even like you. I trusted you, and you threw it in my face."

"I'll make it up to you, I promise," he says, my words not sinking in.

"Shoot him," Esteban orders from his position under the table.

"I've got bigger plans for this asshole," Poker growls.

"Shut up!" Malcolm yells. He takes several steps toward me. "Just shut up!"

Poker moves to stand in front of me. There's about thirty feet of space between me and Malcolm, and I have no doubt that Poker won't let him get any closer than that.

"Call off the dogs, Mistress," Malcolm orders. "Call 'em off, or I'll start shooting."

"You can shoot all you want," I tell him. "But I'm not calling anyone off. Besides, even if I did, do you really think they'd listen when you're pointing a gun at me?"

Malcolm shifts his weapon and points it at Poker. "How about now?"

"Meri, don't even think about it," Poker says quietly. "He's not gonna shoot me."

I don't even have time to blink when Malcolm pulls the trigger, and the bullet hits Poker in the arm. He hisses in pain but doesn't waver.

"That all you got?" Poker taunts.

"Goddammit, P," Crow barks. "Quit while you're ahead."

"I'm not fucking ahead as long as he's got a gun pointed at my woman!"

"Gimme the word, Poker, and I'll take him out," Screamer says from his position.

"No one shoots him," Poker demands. "I want him in the Nightmare Room."

Malcolm pales. "What's the Nightmare Room?" he asks, wavering since the moment he blew his way in here.

I can't see his face, but I know Poker is grinning sadistically. "Use your imagination."

There's a pause, and then Malcolm squares his shoulders, shifting his gun to me. As much as I want to give Poker what he wants, this has to stop. I've already lost Conrad, and my man has already been shot. I can't stand the thought of someone else getting hurt.

"This is the last time I'll ask," Malcolm begins. "Come wi—"

A bullet to his head shuts Malcolm up.

"Who did that?" Poker roars, spinning around to take in all the men. They're all shaking their heads, so he slides his angry gaze to me. "You?"

I shrug before slipping my gun back into the holster. "This had to end. I ended it."

"Dammit, Meri," he seethes.

"Don't," I snap. "I'm not saying this was my fault, but it did happen because of me. It was my job to end it, and I did. I've told you from the beginning that I can take care of myself. Maybe now you'll believe me."

I whirl around to stomp off, but Poker's right there to gather me in his arms.

"I'm sorry, babe," he whispers against my head. "I'm sorry. I just hate the fact that you had to take a life."

I lift my eyes to his. "Have you ever regretted taking the life of someone who's evil?"

"No."

"And I won't either. Malcolm may have been a run-of-the-mill creep, but he was still evil."

"Have I told you today how much I love you?"

I smile. "A few times, but I'm good if you want to keep telling me."

"I'll tell you for the rest of our lives. I love you, Meri. So damn much."

"I love you, too, Poker."

EPILOGUE
POKER

Your happiness is the only thing that matters to me.

One week later...

"She's gonna freak out."

I grin at Screamer as we carry my purchases out of the pet store. Chaos, the Great Dane Meri fell in love with at the animal shelter, is walking regally by my side on his leash. I'm surprised he's being so well behaved because the giant shit is still in his puppy years.

"I can't wait to see her face," I admit. "She's been talking about him nonstop since she shot Malcolm. It was so hard to keep it a secret from her, but I wanted to wait until I knew the fence would be built."

"Where is she today while the guys do that?"

"Addison, Ember, and Wren went with her to see Conrad's family, and then they're taking her for a spa day to hopefully get her to relax a little."

"That'll definitely keep her away from the house long enough," he says. "She already had it partially fenced."

"My thoughts exactly. And if it's not complete before she gets home, we can work on it through the night. I already talked to the guys about it."

"And we'll get the dog door installed, too."

That was the first thing on my list for the pet store. As soon as that was in my cart, I let Chaos lead the way. He's now the proud owner of way more toys than any one dog needs, but I have a feeling it's only the beginning of his life in the lap of luxury.

We get the dog and everything loaded into the club's SUV, and it's not twenty minutes later we're pulling into Meri's driveway.

Our driveway.

I moved in with Meri permanently the day after the shooting. We're adults who know exactly what we want, and that's each other, so why wait?

I clip the leash to Chaos's collar and lead him inside. He drags me through the house toward the back door like he knows exactly where to go. The sliding doors are open to the deck, and I let go of the leash just as he launches himself outside.

"Holy shit," Journey comments with a chuckle. "That's not a puppy, it's a horse."

"Tell me about it," I mutter. "But Meri fell in love with him, and I'd be lying if I'm not halfway there myself."

"Addison called about ten minutes ago," Crow says as he walks toward me. "They'd just left Conrad's house. She said Meri's holding up as well as can be expected. Now they're going to have her pampered. It'll be late by the time they get back."

"Good. I hate that I didn't go with her, but she insisted on going with the old ladies."

"She's gonna be one of them," Journey reminds me. "It's good that she's letting them in like this."

"I know."

During the last week, Meri and I have talked a lot about the future. I blurted out a proposal when she was licking me like a lollipop one night, and as soon as she finished me off, she said 'yes'.

Do I wish I would've done something more romantic? Yes.

Am I upset about the engagement? Absofuckinglutely not.

I have the rest of our lives to give her romance.

Hours pass, and it's not until the sun begins to set that headlights fill the air, and I know my girl is home. The fence was finished twenty minutes ago, so we all head inside, leaving Chaos in the yard.

Don't bark and spoil this.

When Meri steps through the front door, she immediately seeks me out. Her eyes land on me, and her face lights up. She runs, launching herself at me, and I catch her easily.

"Hi," she says.

"Hi. Have a good day?"

"Yeah, for the most part. It was hard with Conrad's family. I set up college funds for the kids and told his wife about them. She was shocked, and I'm not sure she's totally okay with it, but all Conrad wanted was his family taken care of. As soon as I said that, she thanked me."

"It's gonna take her time, but she'll figure out her new normal."

"Yeah."

"How was the spa?"

"Oh my God, it was soooo good."

I make a mental note to ensure she has spa days on the regular. Especially if it puts this look on her face.

"Um, why is everyone here?" she asks me.

"Club business," I lie. "They're all leaving, right guys?"

"Oh, um..." Crow clears his throat. "Sure are. Let's ride, boys!"

"They didn't have to leave," Meri chastises as soon as we're alone.

"Yeah, they did. I've got plans for you, babe."

Her pupils dilate. "You do?"

I grab her hand and drag her to the sliding doors. "I do but close your eyes."

She obeys, and I open the door. Just as I'm guiding her out to the deck, Chaos barks, ruining my grand plan.

Meri squeals, running to the Great Dane, and drops to her knees to roll around in the yard with him.

"Is this for real? Is he really ours?"

"It's real. As of today, Chaos has a forever family."

"Ya hear that, Chaos? You've got a forever family."

The dog barks in response.

"Why do I get the feeling that any other plans I might have had for tonight just got tossed out the window?"

Meri looks over her shoulder and grins. "Because you know I'm not going to be able to stop snuggling this baby. And that's okay, right?"

"Yes, babe, it's okay."

"Good."

I move to sit beside her in the grass. "Are you happy?"

"Deliriously."

"Then fuck plans. Your happiness is the only thing that matters to me."

NEXT IN SOULLESS KINGS MC: MARBLE FALLS, TX
BOOK 5: SCREAMER

Screamer...

My life began the moment I patched in with the Soulless Kings MC. I left all the pain and heartache of my existence behind when I became part of that family, and nothing can make me look at the past or examine the events that scarred my soul... Or so I thought.

When *she* enters my world, I can tell she's built from the same cloth as me. The problem is that her scars also cause the fear she tries so hard to hide. Patience has never been a virtue of mine, but Roxie's testing me in ways that force me to dig deeper than I've ever had to before.

Roxie...

I left Marble Falls for a reason, left the only life I knew to see what else was out there, and all I got for my trouble were bruises and scars that only those who care to look can see. So, I came home, returning to the one place on the planet where I feel a modicum of safety, especially with my brother's motorcycle club at my back.

Trust doesn't come easy for me, especially when it comes to my heart and my Harley, but I'm told that *he* is someone who can help with the latter. Little by little, Screamer uncovers my secrets and teaches me that not all men are horrible, and before I know it, he's the one person who makes me want things I thought were long since impossible.

ALSO BY ANDI RHODES

Broken Rebel Brotherhood

Broken Souls

Broken Innocence

Broken Boundaries

Broken Rebel Brotherhood: Next Generation

Broken Hearts

Broken Wings

Broken Mind

Bastards and Badges

Stark Revenge

Slade's Fall

Jett's Guard

Soulless Kings MC

Fender

Joker

Piston

Greaser

Riker

Trainwreck

Squirrel

Gibson

Flash

Royal

Satan's Legacy MC

Snow's Angel

Toga's Demons

Magic's Torment

Duck's Salvation

Dip's Flame

Devil's Handmaidens MC

Harlow's Gamble

Peppermint's Twist

Mama's Rules

Valhalla Rising MC

Viking

Inferno

Reaper

Mayhem Makers

Forever Savage

Saints Purgatory MC

Unholy Soul

Wrathful Malice

Grim's Hell

Shadowy Abyss

Rogue's Cross

Thorn's Vengeance

Spike's Perdition

Soulless Kings MC: Marble Falls, TX

Crow

Journey

Ghost

ABOUT THE AUTHOR

Andi Rhodes is an author whose passion is creating romance from chaos in all her books! She writes MC (motorcycle club) romance with a generous helping of suspense and doesn't shy away from the more difficult topics. Her books can be triggering for some so consider yourself warned. Andi also ensures each book ends with the couple getting their HEA! Most importantly, Andi is living her real life HEA with her husband and their boxers.